THE DRIVE

YAIR ASSULIN

TRANSLATED FROM THE HEBREW
BY JESSICA COHEN

NEW VESSEL PRESS
NEW YORK

New Vessel Press

www.newvesselpress.com

First published in Hebrew in 2011 as *Neseah*

Copyright © Yair Assulin

Xargol Books and Modan Publishers

Translation Copyright © 2020 Jessica Cohen

Ministry
of Culture
and Sport

With support from "Am Ha-Sefer"—The Israeli Fund for Translation of Hebrew Books,
The Cultural Administration, Israel Ministry of Culture and Sport

Library of Congress Cataloging-in-Publication Data

Assulin, Yair

[Neseah. English]

The Drive/ Yair Assulin; translation by Jessica Cohen.

p. cm.

ISBN 978-1-939931-82-5

Library of Congress Control Number: 2019940460

I. Israel—Fiction

"In the army they don't teach you how to kill;
they teach you how to get killed."
YEHUDA JUDD NE'EMAN

"It is my political right to be a
subject which I must protect."
ROLAND BARTHES

CHAPTER ONE

I.

The Coastal Highway was hazy. The sun had not yet fully risen, and the light that emerged from the mountains and descended to the sea was pale and gray. Dad's face was tired. Soon he would start calling people to cancel meetings. He would apologize, explain that "something came up," say "I have to..." or "I can't make it because..." and pause for a moment, then make up an excuse. I could sense him hiding the fear in his trembling voice, which was weary from a sleepless night. I could sense him trying to project, as he always did, that it was business as usual, "just a little matter of..." When they pressed him and asked if anything was wrong, he insisted that it was nothing serious and signed off with a long "all right" and "take care" and ended the call. Then the car was quiet, a silence that under different circumstances one might have described with pretty words such as "wonderful" or "thought-provoking" or "genuine," but which now was merely the silence of exhaustion and tension gnawing away at one's stomach.

Before leaving Haifa we had the radio on: first Israeli folk songs, then sleepy chatter about the previous day's events. The things that happened yesterday, I thought to myself. And where am I among those things? Why aren't I there? The deep voice on the radio spoke of a woman whose husband had killed her with a knife, stabbed her repeatedly in front of her children, and about Maccabi Haifa who'd won the national championship cup again, and about a Belgian pilot who'd circumnavigated Europe in an airship. Then someone talked about how perhaps a war would break out and perhaps there would be peace, but only perhaps, because at present there were too many factors "hindering progress."

How pathetic, I thought. How stupid. Always some shard of veracity that sneaks in through the back door of the radio and turns into reality for us all: "the news." And what about my reality? What about the reality of last night? I looked at the sea, where the waves were crashing furiously as if they were partners to my pain. Because last night I banged my head against the wall at least fifty times and cried like a baby, and then we stood there in my room, the three of us, Mom and Dad and I, and Dad almost cried, in fact he really did cry, and Mom held him and hugged me, and she too, like me, had cried earlier and her face was damp. Isn't that good enough news for the radio? That's what I thought as I kept looking at the gray sea, which kept crashing against the breakwaters along the coast.

Then I saw a silver-colored car parked by the beach, and for a few moments I allowed myself to imagine the couple that might have been sitting inside it. Her head was probably resting on his lap or belly, and the seats were probably pushed back, almost all the way down, and she was whispering to him that she loved him, or the other way around, being quiet while he told her he loved her. Or perhaps he'd already told her that too many times, I thought, and I imagined her saying nothing upon hearing those words that he repeated over and over again in order to hear an answer that never came. And then I thought of Ayala. I can't remember what state we were in back then, when I took that drive. It was a long time ago, and it had been unclear for quite some time whether we were really together or just stuck in a distant relationship that sometimes felt like a body slung over my back and at other times like the only thing that existed in the world. And how seldom were the times when it seemed like the only thing in the world.

I remembered that night we slept in my mom's car at Lake Kinneret; I remembered the sun beating down on my face in the morning and my headache that got worse and worse, like a nightmare, when I kept turning my head back and forth, trying to get away from the sun and sleep a little longer—anything but wake up. I remembered how at some point I gave up on sleep and opened the door to breathe in the fresh air. And then I saw her standing there on the shore, wrapped in a white blanket, gazing at the water. It was hot, and the sun had already risen quite far, but the sky was gray exactly as it was on that drive with Dad: a sky the sickly color of faded work pants. We stood there looking out at the water together, silently, and after that we broke up for a few weeks.

I remembered a conversation we had before I joined the army. She said she was afraid I'd go crazy, that our relationship would die when I was in the army because we'd stop being together. Then I remembered that we had that conversation right here, just outside Haifa, near the spot where I saw the car parked by the beach. I think there was a sand sculpture competition on the beach that day, and we went to see a statue of Buddha that everyone was talking about—a fat, smiling Buddha. I remember Ayala in big, black sunglasses, holding my hand, or perhaps it would be more accurate to say that I was holding her hand, and she talked about how afraid she was, without looking at me.

"Maybe we should end it now, before you go into the army," she said. "You understand that afterward it'll be a lot more painful, for both of us." She always pulled out those clichés and said them with a serious expression, the sort of lines that gave her that Tel-Aviv-New-York-intellectual tone that she was so fond of, like a character in a Woody Allen film, always in a confident voice, the kind used by someone who knows everything.

I was also decisive when we talked on the beach. I also used pretty words and talked about "love" and "coping with crises" and what we "need" and what we "don't need." But that morning, when I took the drive with Dad, sitting next to him in the car with my knees clasped together like a little girl who has to go potty, I derided myself for being so decisive, and for the clichés. "If we really love each other, that should be enough, shouldn't it?" I asked her. "How can we break up when we love each other? Are you saying we're going to break up every time things get hard? There are always situations like this in life, like the army. And if you love me the way you say you do, then we have to go on. Besides, everyone gets through it, don't they? Are you saying everyone who goes into the army just gives up everything?"

What arrogance, I thought on that drive, to talk about the army as if it were something familiar, something known, something "everyone goes through." I admonished myself: Had you ever been through anything like the army when you said those words to her? I found solace in a segment of orange that Dad handed me as he drove, and in his face, which contained, beyond disappointment and sadness, the familiar lines of love. Have you ever even been in that situation, or one like it? A situation in which your desire doesn't matter at all, where you're constantly being told what to do, when to eat and when to sleep and when to run and when to talk on the phone, and even when you're allowed to take a shit or a piss?

I remember my first month in the army, in basic training, when I was on the bus with my platoon sergeant and I didn't know if I was allowed to eat a piece of candy I had in my pocket, because they told us we weren't allowed to eat any-thing without permission, not even candy. I remember that I deliberated for a long time about whether or not he would notice me eating it, and what would happen if he did. My desire to take comfort in the candy, coupled with my fear of being punished if he caught me eating it without permission, drove me to ask him if I was allowed to. I can hear my fragile voice, my failure to comprehend that this sergeant was only slightly older than I was, and that he too was a soldier who just wanted to finish his service and go back to being a nor-mal human being. "Sergeant, can I have a candy?" I asked. "No. Why would you?" he answered immediately in his cut-ting, nasal voice. I think again about my arrogance before enlisting, about the entirely unfounded confidence, perhaps even the repression of what was about to happen, and again I am filled with the shame of failure.

And I think about Ayala again. Her face was thin back then, and I remember her prominent cheekbones, her short black hair and white skin, her lips pursed dubiously when we talked on the beach that day, among the statues, when I said that the army was something everyone had to get through so we shouldn't make such a big deal out of it, and that love was the most important thing. Then I remember her kissing me.

II.

Dad turned the radio back on. I remember how once, when I was in elementary school, he picked me up from one of those after-school activities I used to enthusiastically sign up for at the beginning of every year and stop going to after a few times, and he taught me a biblical verse: "Let not him that girdeth on his armor boast himself as he that putteth it off." To this day I can hear him explaining what those words meant, and the story sounded so wonderful to me: "'Him that girdeth on his armor' is the soldier preparing for war, who doesn't know if he is going to win or lose. And 'he that putteth it off' is the soldier who comes back from war after winning." I remember picturing a soldier going off to battle, like King Saul, and a soldier returning triumphantly, like David. In those days I knew "David's Lament for Saul and Jonathan" by heart, and each evening I would ask Mom to read it to me from the Children's Bible. I think of how my soul thrilled every time I heard anything about armies and wars and victories.

Now the word *army* makes me nauseous. I remember the many occasions when Dad reminded me of that verse. One of the last was when I talked about how I was going to become an outstanding warrior, and I pictured myself with my buzz cut and my brawny body, marching through all sorts of dark places, and the glory that would follow, especially among women.

Once, just to see her eyes fill with worry, I even described to Mom how the notification officer would knock on our door at two a.m. to inform them of my death. She got mad and yelled at me to stop. I didn't just do it to Mom, I also did it to Shlomit, whom I loved very much at the time, and for the same exact purpose: to see the worry flood her blue eyes. And I remember Dad telling me in a reproachful voice: "How many times must I recite that verse for you? 'Let not him that girdeth on his armor boast himself as he that putteth it off.'"

III.

The car coasted along the empty highway to the Mental Health Officer at Tel Hashomer Hospital. "Tell me what you want," Dad had said the night before, in tears, after I'd cried for perhaps an hour without stopping and said I couldn't go on, that I felt as if I were suffocating, that I'd rather die than go back to the base. "Just tell me what you want," he repeated, "what do you want to do? What do you want to happen?"

"I don't know," I answered. "I don't know, I really don't. I just know that I don't want to go back there. I don't want to."

"But what is it that's so terrible there?" he asked for the millionth time since I'd first cried over the phone, and I knew that someone looking from the outside could not even begin to comprehend the suffocation that filled me each time I took the train to the base, the insurmountable pain I felt when I walked through those gates, the fear of something I cannot describe or define, the horribly cramped sensation that was unrelated to anything, certainly not to a particular place or space. Again I told him that I was miserable. Again I told him that I felt I was losing myself. A few days earlier I'd told him I wanted to jump in front of oncoming traffic. I didn't want to die, I just wanted some time off, a little time to calm down.

Now I remember that picture clearly, of how I stood on the side of the dilapidated road outside the base and there was mud everywhere. I remember the headlights of a distant car approaching, and the feeling that this time I was serious, this time I was really going to do it. I remember the voices in my head that told me I'd already said that so many times, and I remember the insistence in my mind that this time I had no choice, I was going to jump, and even if I died I didn't care. Then I envisioned Mom and Dad's faces, and I heard Mom's voice, which had been slightly high-pitched when I'd called a few days or a week earlier and burst into tears when I said I couldn't take it anymore.

I was on a different base then, near Nablus. The whole unit was on that base, which was full of tents and surrounded by giant concrete walls, long lines of massive gray blocks. I walked around for a week feeling as if I were going to suffocate. All I wanted to do was shut my eyes and sleep. It was winter and the work was exhausting: sitting in the war room listening to the phone. It wasn't dangerous, I know, not dangerous like driving in the middle of the night in a black Audi to arrest a wanted person in a village, or like sitting at a lookout post in the middle of nowhere when someone could put a bullet through your head at any minute, or like actually fighting in Lebanon or Gaza. But for me, it was soul-crushing. It wasn't just the work but all the people who hung around those big rooms full of telephones and supposedly important conversations, and the horrible feeling that you were insignificant. That you were nothing. That you were but one more instrument on the desk, like the pen or the computer or the old, encoded phones. Sometimes I had the feeling that I wasn't even an instrument, that in fact I hardly existed, that I had to do everything for someone who did everything for someone who did everything for someone, and sometimes I had the feeling that the ladder never ended but merely branched out endlessly and reeked and grew mold and became caked with mud.

That was how I felt on that base, but I know that even that doesn't explain the phone call when I could no longer suppress my sobs as soon as I heard my mother ask how I was. Up until then I kept trying to sound as if everything was fine, there was no problem, I was doing all right. And that definitely was not a reason I could give Dad when he asked me, "What's so bad there?" Because even that didn't explain why things were so bad for me there—not the reeking ladder that never ended or the fact that I wasn't important and didn't exist, not even the dreadful fact that I did not have my own regular bed on that base, that a few of us shared what was called a "whore bed," and every morning I had to strip my sheets off and shove them under the bunk bed in the big green dusty bag we were given at the induction center. Or that after a night shift I had to wait for someone to get up so that I could get some sleep until they came to wake me up and tell me I'd slept enough, or in fact not even wake me, because I was usually awake already and lying in bed with my eyes closed just to steal a few more moments of quiet, a few seconds in which I could think about Ayala, for example, and remember how a few weeks ago we'd had a wonderful conversation after we hadn't talked for a while, or to think about the argument I'd had with Dror and about how I was right—to reanalyze the logic of my position and verify that I really was right. That was probably also not the reason for the phone call that dropped us into the whirlwind that eventually saved my life.

And yes, I know that every soldier goes through similar things at one time or another, and there are some who go through much worse, and there are even some who are going through similar things right now, as I write these words in a quiet room, with a Schubert sonata for violin and piano playing in the background. But when your soul hurts—and in those days it hurt more than I had ever imagined it could, and it kept on hurting more and more—all this knowledge about other people and other pain makes no difference and offers no relief.

IV.

In the end I didn't jump. Something gripped me by the calves and would not let me take that leap forward. I remember standing as the car passed me and kept going, unaware of the enormous role it would have been destined to play had I jumped. Then I thought about this matter of fate, and about how if I had jumped I might have died, and the driver might have gone to prison without truly being at fault.

I imagined the face of an army driver I knew. I imagined him as the driver of the car that had just gone by, and I imagined that I had jumped and he'd hit me. I imagined his face when he got out of the car to see what he'd hit, and his mouth opening to shout for help. I imagined his face at the inquiry and then in court, and I remembered a Rashi parable about an accidental murderer and a malicious murderer and how everything in the world falls into place, because "a reward shall be brought about by a meritorious person and a debt by the debtor," but I couldn't decide if by me not jumping, thereby preventing him from hitting me, he would end up with merit or debt. All these musings went through my mind in no longer than a few seconds, because immediately afterward, when I realized that now I had to go back to the barracks full of pathetic soldiers and officers who only cared about covering their own asses, I was once again flooded with that terrible feeling of suffocation and shortness of breath, and I prayed that another car would go by, but none did, the road remained dark. I headed back toward the barracks. I think it started raining and I hid under the asbestos shelter of a weapons depot.

V.

In fact I never shared the preoccupation with these things called "army" and "values," or with the dubious glory of "defending the homeland." It is true that when I was a boy I liked to picture myself as a magnificent warrior with a hefty body, and I even imagined recounting to everyone at Friday night dinners what we'd done that week, or not recounting but sitting there proudly silent so that everyone would understand that "there are things best left unsaid." When I forecasted my own death and how the army notification officer would come knock on the door, I enjoyed watching the sorrow fill Mom's eyes and fill me with stupid conceit until she yelled at me to stop. But when I got older it simply passed, the way all kinds of childish thoughts you don't fully understand pass. That was before I really knew what the army was and what the whole story was. I understood all the clichés people used to explain it, but I no longer believed in them. And because I was no longer part of the military story by the time I got to high school, when everyone talked about commando units and how they were working out so they'd be ready for service—some kids didn't just talk but went running on the beach or did all kinds of treks with weights strapped to their legs "to improve endurance"—I looked down on it, and I said I was positive the army knew how to prepare its soldiers and there was nothing stupider than starting military service before it really started. But even though I'd always known that the whole business with the army and values and defending your homeland was a big show, it was only in the car that day, when the two of us were driving to the MHO, while Dad searched for a pen in the ashtray next to the gearshift to write something down about a postponed meeting, did it suddenly become very clear to me, clearer than all the times I had considered it previously, that no one really believed in those lofty concepts, and that all the talk about protecting the homeland and giving back to the country was the empty rhetoric of people seeking respect.

I remember my enlistment day. I think it was the saddest day of my life, at least up until that point, because afterward my life began to sink and rapidly lost color. We went to a concert the night before, and even then I could already feel the contractions in my belly, which were pretty similar to what I used to feel every year in the last few days of summer vacation. The feeling that what little time was left was already lost, because it was entirely devoted to the bad things lurking around the corner. The music was wonderful and Ayala and I held hands throughout the show. There was a sense of grace, and I did not understand—or perhaps I understood but did not translate the understanding into thought—that the grace would be followed by a heavy toll. When I woke up the next morning I did not want to get out of bed. My hair was cut short and my face shaved, and my gear was arranged in a backpack that sat next to the mirror. I looked at the books on the shelf, then at the CDs in a metal rack next to the stereo system, and I felt terrible. Dad, who woke me up, was also hesitant. He said the big day had arrived, then he quipped that I should remember that the really hard part was the thirty years of reserve duty after my regular service.

I washed my face and looked at myself in the mirror. I remembered how Nir had told me that the day before he enlisted he went into the bathroom at the Haifa mall and burst into tears. He just sat there on the filthy floor and sobbed. "For at least half an hour," he told me. I wanted to cry too. Horrible pressure filled my windpipe. Then Mom, Dad, Tal, Galia and I left the house, and we drove to the central bus station in Haifa.

I remember now, as I remembered then, on that drive to the MHO with Dad, how the Egged buses were all lined up. I also remember Ayala and Dror and Michal and some other people who came to see me off. Some of the girls there were very beautiful, and there were lots of boys playing at being real men because they were joining the army, so they hugged their girlfriends with one arm that was muscular and puffed up from training. There were parents who had only to give those boys a single look to remind them that they were still children. And there were friends looking forward to the day they enlisted, or dreading it but turning the fear into fake happiness for the sake of whoever was joining up. There were some who were already in the army and knew all the time what was going to happen, including a few who plainly evinced suffering in almost every move they made, and others who'd already turned into part of the machine called "the army" and talked about it admiringly.

VI.

First we waited downstairs, on the same floor as the restaurants, all of which except one bakery were closed because it was so early. Dad asked me if I wanted something to eat. "Maybe *bourekas* or a croissant? I'll bring you something with coffee." But I couldn't eat and I said I wasn't hungry: "What I had at home was fine." Dad said that was okay, he was pretty sure they'd give us lunch after we got to the induction center: "You never go hungry in the army," he promised. When I think about those words now, I try to recall a single meal throughout my military service where I left feeling full. It is true that some people would eat anything, even chicken drumsticks with bread or tasteless spaghetti with bread, and they left full. But I'd always been a picky eater and I was never able to eat the way they did, and I always left hungry. After particularly greasy lunches, I also had heartburn.

After standing around for about half an hour in the food court where everything except the bakery was shuttered, trying to chatter like everyone else, as if everything was the same as usual and all of us boys standing around with our buzz cuts and close shaves were going on a school trip, and people kept offering advice or asking if I'd taken this thing and if I hadn't forgotten the other thing, we went upstairs into a big room where a soldier was reading out the names of all the draftees. On the way to the MHO, the memory of that scene suddenly shocked me. I remembered that soldier, who was roughly my age and was sending me off to three years of slow death. In those moments, while I waited for my name to be called, everything mingled inside me. On the one hand I wanted that damn soldier to call my name already, and for the waiting to be over so that the cursed three-year clock could start ticking. I was tired of all the looks I kept encountering, from my parents and the other people who were smiling at me as if they were silently reciting stupid platitudes like "what a great nation we are," or "such sacrifice," or "where else do young people serve their country before going to university?" I wanted the lie to end and the smiles to be wiped away and the army to begin. But on the other hand, with every moment that passed without my name being called, I breathed a sigh of relief, because perhaps in some unconscious way I thought that each moment when my name was not called was another moment in which I could escape, another moment in which I could stand up on one of the metal benches and scream that I didn't want to go anywhere, that I didn't want to be a soldier.

Every few minutes I glanced at Ayala. Sometimes she looked beautiful and sometimes horribly ugly. She stood there with a knowing look, as if to say, "I told you so" before anything had even happened. As though she could already see the future that I could not yet see, with the pain that would come, the phone calls late into the night, the crying, the end of our relationship.

After a few minutes they called my name. Like all the other names, mine was called by that soldier, who I only now understand was around my age, wearily doing his job and waiting for the day to be over without paying attention to the repercussions of what came out of his mouth. Everyone hugged me quickly, and Ayala, who was wearing jeans and the cutoff shirt she'd worn the first time we met, gave me an especially close hug. I loved her very much at that moment. I remember that Michal cried. She's the kind of person who always does what you're supposed to do exactly when you're supposed to do it. Dror hugged me, and I think Michael did too. Then my dad came over and told me it wasn't easy, but everyone did it and he'd done it too, and he believed I could do it. Mom and Tal and Galia wished me luck. Mom cried when she hugged me.

VII.

When I was a boy, and sometimes it still happens today, I used to reconstruct situations I'd been in that had led to bad things, and I'd think about what I should have done differently. I particularly remember doing that after I got into fights with kids who were stronger than me and made me surrender, and then, in bed before falling asleep, I would reconsider where and when I should have given them a kick or a punch that would have finished them off. I would imagine them lying on the floor, begging for mercy, while the other kids, who in reality had made fun of me, stood there marveling at my strength. That's how I would imagine myself to sleep. That's also what happened with that enlistment scene, when they called my name and I said good-bye and walked to the bus with my backpack on my shoulder; the evening before, I'd crammed it full of all the items on the list they'd sent me in a brown envelope with a red stamp from the State of Israel and the Israel Defense Forces.

I ran that scene through my mind many times, and tried to imagine what I should have done differently. I imagined that I pretended to get on the bus but at the last minute I went around the back and disappeared, then ran to the sea, which was walking distance from the station, and hid under a big rock just like Dad did when he was a little boy and they tried to shave his head and douse him with disinfectant.

Even though I knew there was no chance of getting away from that monster, the army, in my imagination I succeeded. I imagined how I ran away, and how I hid on the beach and went home after a few hours, and Mom, in the kitchen, was surprised to see me back and asked what had happened, and I told her that in the end they didn't need me, they'd let me go, and that I was tired and going to sleep, and she smiled and accepted what I told her as if it made sense, and went back to cooking.

VIII.

Dad stopped the car on the side of the road and got out to wash his face. When we'd left home it was still dark, too early to say the dawn prayers, so Dad said we would pray "when we get this business over with." He took a bottle out of the trunk and splashed his face with water. There was a cool breeze and I zipped up my army fleece jacket. My feet hurt and I saw flocks of birds flying over the *moshav* we'd stopped outside. I was wearing an army shirt, untucked, and army pants that covered the red boots because I hadn't secured them with elastic bands. I looked at Dad. He saw my look and put his hand on mine. I told him I was sorry, and he said there was nothing to be sorry about, that he knew I was telling the truth, but all he was saying, again, was that he could not understand what was so bad for me there, and that he thought or feared I wasn't telling him everything, because if I was then he simply could not understand why it was so bad.

"Are you getting three meals a day?" he asked. "Are you sleeping? Are you showering? Because if so, then I really cannot understand what's so bad there." He paused for a few moments and then asked if I was being abused, "because if you are, tell me, and then I can understand, then we can take care of it. Answer me, are you being abused?"

I remember his eyes narrowing and widening as he talked, and I remember thinking about how I must have inherited my oratorical skills from him, those methods for getting your listeners' attention and riveting them to what you're saying, like narrowing and widening your eyes. I had the same exact thought the night before the drive, when he came up to my room after I'd banged my head against the wall repeatedly, and Tal, whose room shared a wall with mine, had asked me what was going on, and when I couldn't stop crying she'd run to call him and Mom. I remember his slippers gently flapping up the stairs and Mom behind him. I didn't know what to tell them but I knew they had to see me in that state because it was the only way they would understand that I was really crashing. I remember that he hugged me, and Mom sat down on the edge of the bed.

"First of all, calm down," he said. Then he asked me what I wanted to do, and all I could say, over and over again, was that I didn't want to go back. Then he asked, or perhaps it was Mom who asked, if I was being abused.

IX.

No, I wasn't being abused, and I honestly did not know how to explain my condition. What I did tell them was only because I had to say something that would sound like a reasonable explanation for my mental state. I repeated that the army was suffocating me. I said that all around the world, this was the age when a person should be flourishing, and I felt as if I were dying in the army. Why did we Israelis have to do that? I said I was dying, that I couldn't breathe in that place.

"But why?" Dad kept asking, over and over again. He could not understand, or rather, he refused to understand, this thing that had been present in me all those years but had now become impossible to ignore: that I was, apparently, not like everyone else. Not like all the people who just decide to do the army and then do it, and no matter how bad things are, they still get up every morning and go. Some even turn their suffering into a principle and milk it for the respect that stupid people give them and the stories they can tell their friends on weekends and at family gatherings. Many of them even come to believe that the army is a "formative experience," that it's "wonderful," that it "builds character." What stupidity.

I have never understood how people can make a principle out of suffering, especially in the army, where I felt that nobody really cared about me and whether or not I was making a contribution, as long as they could climb over my back and suck my blood for their glory or their rank or even a few words of praise. Dad said I had to learn to be more flexible, not to demand perfection from everything and everyone. But the truth is that I don't demand perfection. Not even close. I simply ask that every person be what he demands from others. Just that.

I remember one soldier from my intelligence unit, who would always—especially on operations that were notorious for lousy conditions—exploit a back problem he once had and complain about pain, so that he could get sick leave and stay home. Everyone would get mad at him and curse "that asshole who always shafts us," and I would just sit quietly to the side, because I knew that every one of them would do the exact same thing if given the chance. And how infuriating and disappointing that the one time I got sick leave and had to go home—and it was a justified sick leave—it was that guy, of all people, who came over to me with his big nose and his blue eyes and told me I was "shafting everyone and he was sick as fuck of it." I didn't say anything, but that night in bed I thought I should have screamed at him and told him he was the last person who could say something like that and that he was a big fuck himself.

X.

Dad finished washing his face and got back into the car. I sat down a few minutes later, after standing outside a while longer looking out at the moshav, with chicken coops stretching all the way from the highway to the houses, and thin, bare trees in the middle. I hated that landscape. I hated the stench that was already rising from it in this early morning hour, filling the air. I looked at a house where a light was on, and I thought about Ayala. She'd called me a few times the night before but I hadn't answered. Every so often she calls me and talks about how hard it is for her that we're together but not together, and yesterday I was tired and did not have the strength to get into all that again. Then Dad gave a little honk and jerked his head at me to get in. He signaled left and merged into traffic, which was picking up now.

I put a Leonard Cohen CD on and listened quietly to the first song. I remembered a conversation Ayala and I had about a month before, when I was trying to decide whether or not to see the MHO. I told her I was afraid of the asinine way people looked at anyone who'd been to the MHO, as if they were crazy or a menace to society, or at best a despicable shirker who refused to give back to the country that had raised him and protected him and cared for him. Then I told her that in our religious community, where everyone knew everything about one another, the whole business of stigmatizing people who get mental health exemptions was especially bad, and that she couldn't do anything about it because that was the society I'd been born into, and the fact that I wanted to live a religious lifestyle forced me to stay in contact with it to some degree, and to tolerate its negative aspects.

I remembered that we sat in the car while we talked. We were on the coast. I did not look at her but at the empty, black beach. I don't remember if it was raining that evening, but I remember the strong winds that rocked the palm trees they'd just planted along the beach. I talked more and more about my pain; I'd never talked about my pain that much. Once in a while I stopped the flow of speech and sat silently for several moments. I remembered saying, "I'm scared that I won't be able to get married," and that sentence echoed in my mind. I remembered that I looked at her, at her black hair and white skin. We probably kissed after that, I'm not sure. I remembered that she stroked my face and said the problem was solved because "I'll always be there for you."

How pathetic words are, I thought in the car on the way to the MHO, while Dad hummed "Suzanne" along with Leonard Cohen. A year ago, I called Ayala and she wouldn't talk to me. "I want to erase you," she told me, and awhile later I saw her with a guy I used to know a little, and they were kissing. "I'll always be there for you." I play that sentence over and over in my mind. I don't love her anymore, and if I'm being honest, it's doubtful I ever did. But that betrayal of words, the capacity of people to say things without really meaning them, or to say things and take them back, or even to say them and deny they'd ever said them—that betrayal drives me mad. I think, sadly, that I might need to let go of my naiveté about words, which makes me believe what people say.

CHAPTER TWO

_____I._____

Now in my room, the times commingle. Only that drive to the MHO with Dad remains, like a spine running down the whole time period. I remember one night when Ayala and I stood in a big parking lot and she yelled at me that I didn't understand her. That she couldn't talk to me. That there was no point in talking with me. I remember that I threw up all night afterward. Ayala was a very commanding figure throughout that whole era of "my army." I don't know if that's where our decline began, or if there were a few little stones thrown in our path even before I enlisted. But it's clear that the whole period of joining the army, the depression, the madness of banging my head against the wall, standing on the side of the road thinking about jumping in front of a car, and my strong desire for absolute silence—all that was a very significant blow to our relationship.

I remember that once I cried in front of her. She encouraged me to cry. She stroked my head and talked about how good it was to cry. I remember her face before we said goodbye that night. It felt as though after she'd seen me broken, after she'd seen me weak, a layer of distance had formed in her, as if I repulsed her. I remember now that one of the first times we went out, when we sat close together on an almost completely vacant floor of a shopping mall and our hands linked for the first time, she looked at me with that look of hers and asked me to promise never to hurt her. At the time I was the strong one, the one who had the power to hurt. Now it seems to me that my crash in the damn army, more than a year later, simply disappointed her. Perhaps more than that. Perhaps she felt that I'd betrayed her. I'd promised to be strong and I turned out to be weak and helpless. Suddenly I was crying in front of her and she was the one stroking my head.

When Dad and I drove to the MHO, I didn't tell anyone I was going. Even after returning, it took me awhile to say that I'd been to the mental health services. I don't know why, but my shame over that trip, over the pain I felt, which was genuine, prevented me from telling people. Or perhaps it was not the shame but the fear that they wouldn't understand the way things really were and would think I was lying or being spoiled. The fear that someone at synagogue who heard about it would come up to me and say, in a very understanding tone of voice, that "even though it was hard for all of us, we all got through it." And then he'd give me a pitiful look and say, "It's for your future, see? In Israel these days, people who don't do the army can't get by on the outside." And then he'd stick his fat face in mine, right into my eyes that were still puffy from crying at home a few hours or days earlier, and he'd put his hand on my shoulder.

I would keep thinking about that line, "It's for your future," and about all the lofty talk of ideals and values and every person's obligation to serve the homeland and all those slogans, and about how in fact the army had nothing to do with values. About how everyone who does their military service does it only because if they don't, they can't get by "on the outside," and that's how the world works. And if people who didn't serve in the army could get along "on the outside" then it would be okay not to want to serve in the army. Lots of people wouldn't want to. And then I would remember the pitiful look from the man at synagogue, and I'd feel the disgust, and I'd think about how everyone thought I was lying.

And to be honest, why shouldn't they think I was lying? After all, everyone lies. They lie about everything, including the army. Everyone's lying—even the ones who go to the MHO and make up hallucinations and visions and then tell their friends how they pulled one over on the MHO and how the idiot gave them exactly what they wanted. And the ones who go home after a week of dreary guard duty and tell everyone heroic tales as if they're carrying the whole State of Israel on their shoulders, the whole Zionist dream. So why wouldn't they think I was lying? Why wouldn't they think I was a liar just like everyone else? I kept wondering that. Over and over and over again. Even though I was actually not lying.

II.

Now I remember a conversation, which I recalled that day on the way to the MHO too with my platoon commander, who was a lieutenant colonel. But I also remember the first time I saw him. It was my first day in the platoon. He'd arrived that evening from a different base, and we were sitting on a bench by the square. I remember he had a small yarmulke perched on the side of his head, and he was fat, with fleshy but dry lips that threatened to spill out, and he was spewing curses and talking about sex. I recognized him as soon as I saw him. He was one of those types you meet for only a minute but they get lodged in your memory forever, for no reason, or at least not a conscious one.

He'd been a substitute teacher when I was in elementary school, but he'd taught us only one class. He had celiac disease, and I remember how he explained to us what celiac was and what gluten was, and what could happen if he ate bread or cake or anything else with that stuff in it. I remember that he spread his arms alongside his fat body and acted as if he were exploding. Because, he said, with a simplicity that I found frightening, if he ate bread he would simply explode. I remember how I imagined all the classroom walls stained with his blood and pieces of his skin. Then he told us he wanted to join the army but the army wouldn't let him because it couldn't provide him with the kind of bread he was allowed to eat. He said he was going to fight until they broke down and let him serve.

I remember that I felt sorry for him that day, in class, when he stood there with his arms to the sides, pretending he was going to explode. I remembered him fondly. He was nice in that one single class he taught us, and I was happy when I realized he was going to be my commander. It never occurred to me what a filthy, destructive, power-hungry man he really was. Sometimes I suffer from naiveté: I see human beings' pitiful aspects before anything else, and I feel sorry for them, and my pity for their lousy fates makes me perceive them as good people. The next day, on the way to dinner, with the innocence of a new soldier who thinks the army is one more place in reality where you can act the way you do anywhere else, I knocked on his office door and told him that I remembered him from that one class, and I remembered him explaining about the celiac and the gluten and how the army wouldn't let him enlist. He just laughed, with his disgusting mouth and the goiter on his neck, and said we were stupid kids and we'd driven him crazy.

I didn't think that was true, and when I left his office I was sad. I went to dinner alone, because no one was waiting for me, and I felt like a kid whose childhood hero had been destroyed. Like a little boy who goes backstage after a show and meets the actors who play his childhood heroes, and finds that they are repulsive, crass people who are nothing like the characters they portray. He bore no resemblance to the character I'd seen in my mind. He was a repulsive human being—something I came to understand increasingly over time.

III.
_____

The evening when I had to go and talk with him followed a long and unsuccessful effort to overcome my emotional pain and restlessness, and a difficult night when I actually burst into tears. It happened after we came back to our regular base from the base near Nablus. I remember that evening almost entirely. It might have been the most significant evening of my service, one that arguably led to me and Dad eventually taking that early morning drive, after a long and sleepless night, to see the MHO at Tel Hashomer.

I remember that I was working in the war room they'd set up on our base because of some operation that had already started or was about to start, which we had to prepare for. I remember the oppressive feeling I'd had that day, a feeling that carried on its back all the harsh feelings of the preceding days.

It was my shift, and I was laminating maps of cities in the West Bank. I wanted to get out of there. A female petty officer who was connected to the Intelligence platoon was sitting in the war room with me and another soldier—I can't remember who, or even whether it was a man or a woman. I do remember the officer's ugly face, her black hair that made me think of pubic hair, and her faint moustache. I remember her eyes and her crushed nose. But more than any of those features, I remember with disgust the self-importance that dripped from her, just like the sweat that covered her armpits and dripped down her arms while she sat on a plastic chair that was about to break. I remember that she leaned back and played with her frizzy hair, and gave us a condescending, self-important look. And just like with the lieutenant colonel, I thought back to the first time I'd seen her.

It was when I joined the platoon after they transferred me from the combat unit because they discovered I had asthma. I'd always had it, but when I told the doctor at the recruiting office that I was asthmatic, he sent me to get my lungs tested, and afterward I saw a doctor who just smiled and said I had "the lungs of a lion." But when the asthma was finally diagnosed, the placement officer sent me to Intelligence. "Ask for Gali," she told me, "she'll be your officer." When I heard that name, Gali, I pictured a beautiful woman. I imagined how I would join the platoon and make her fall in love with me, and we'd walk around the base, which looked like a pretty nice place when I first got there, and we'd talk and laugh, and I'd hold her close to me and she'd whisper in my ear how lucky it was that I'd ended up in her platoon because . . .

But when I saw her, the real Gali, the one whom the placement officer had said would be my officer, sitting on a bench outside the office writing something in a notebook, all my fantasies vanished and I was filled with revulsion. And that day in the war room, while I laminated maps, I thought back to that first time I'd seen her after picturing her as someone completely different.

IV.
_____

A few hours before I went into the war room, I talked to Mom on the phone. I told her I couldn't take it anymore. I told her, again, that I was unhappy, that I felt as if I were suffocating, that I had to get out of that place. She said she would talk to my commander, the lieutenant colonel, and we'd see what could be done. I know it sounds like I was just whining, because nothing that bad had happened to me, but I write these words now, and I intend to write them again and again: I really could not tolerate it. My soul was genuinely threatening to explode at any moment. I really wanted to die. Every morning I wanted to die when I woke up and saw that miserable, gray room with its four bunk beds, and the other soldiers getting dressed and polishing their boots, and I realized that another horribly normal day was about to begin. During the lousy week before I talked to my mom and she talked to the lieutenant colonel and she told me to go see him because he said he'd talk to me and would try to help me however he could, I stood on the side of the road several times, right near the passing cars, and planned to jump. I swore I would jump. But over and over again, the image of Mom and Dad stopped me and paralyzed my legs.

In fact, I will now write something even harsher: since my time in the army, I am no longer afraid of death. I was suffering so much that death became a presence in my life, a logical option for escape, a solution. Death became my second shadow. Like a comrade in arms who could betray me at any moment and dig his sword into my back, but as long as he hadn't done that, he was my friend.

Anyway, when I was kneeling on the floor in the war room, laminating another map of some village that Gali told me to laminate, my cell phone rang, and Mom told me she'd talked to my commander and he'd said I should go see him after my shift and he'd have a talk with me and see what was going on and how to help.

"What was he like?" I asked her. There were tears in my eyes, as there were every time I talked to her back then.

"He was fine," she said, "he was very nice. He immediately said he'd try to help however he could."

"Are you sure?" I thought about that stupid statement, 'however he could.'

"He sounded very nice to me," she repeated. "I hope it'll work out, I hope he can help you."

She herself was skeptical about talks with commanders by then. She'd already talked at least three times with Dan, the first lieutenant, who was the officer more directly responsible for the soldiers and was also the lieutenant colonel's deputy. Dan had called me in for a few talks but nothing had come of it. Generally speaking, Mom found my whole situation in the army unfamiliar. I remember that she once told me, on the first Shabbat when I came home after crying on the phone, when I was on that base full of tents surrounded by fucking concrete walls, that when her friends were in the army there was no such thing as not wanting to go back to the base, and anyone who wanted to be transferred had to submit a request and would get a response only after a few months, and it was usually negative.

"Did you know there were a lot more soldiers who committed suicide back then?" I asked her. "And there were soldiers who defected and went AWOL, weren't there?"

She looked at me worriedly. "Are you thinking about suicide?"

"I'm not thinking about anything," I answered, and she said that things weren't as they used to be anyway, and these days anyone who doesn't want to do the army doesn't do it, and the most important thing is for me to feel well.

I don't remember what I told her on the phone after she said the lieutenant colonel had sounded nice and she hoped he could help me, or how the conversation ended. I remember only the feeling I had—perhaps relief, or hope, that maybe the solution lay in this meeting. What the solution would be, I did not know. I didn't know if I just wanted to leave that goddamn base, or if I wanted to serve close to home, or leave the whole rotten army altogether.

"Maybe I should put my head out the window and scream that I hate the whole army?" I said to Dad as we drove to the MHO.

"Stop your nonsense already," he said, "because you do understand. You understand that without the IDF this country could not exist."

"But how does it exist now?" I retorted. "It has laws requiring eighteen-year-olds to enlist, it takes their best years, all their dreams, it destroys their souls, teaches them that what matters is cheating and stealing and trampling and cutting corners and occupying and winning. Is that what a state should teach people at this age? Does that strike you as normal?"

"You're exaggerating," Dad said.

"I'm not," I answered, with a vehemence that suddenly spilled out of me after a sleepless night. "That's exactly how it is. That's what they teach, don't you see that?"

We drove on in silence, and my thoughts returned to that conversation with the lieutenant colonel who disgusts me every time I think of him. I remembered again the good feeling I had after talking with Mom, a feeling that was completely washed out of me when I went back into the war room and Gali told me I was talking on the phone too much, and that maybe I should stop disappearing and start helping out a little.

I wanted to shout at her, really scream at the top of my lungs, but the only thing that came out was a whimper. Then I sat down on a chair and stared into space, holding back the tears.

"Will you stop with the drama?" she said, and I wanted to yell again. I wanted to ask her who she thought she was, to tell her to shut her stinking mouth already and go wash the sweat stains off her armpits and shave off her disgusting moustache. To go fuck herself.

But I didn't say anything. Throughout that whole period, my entire military service, I had a fear of people who could judge me and punish me and leave me on the base for a weekend or even put me in prison. I felt powerless against them. My soul, sometimes fully coercing my brain, would not allow me to yell at them or reproach them, and so my most important capacity was severed—my capacity to express myself. My genuine ability to speak. And that's how it was at my meeting with the lieutenant colonel, which I'd looked forward to so desperately after my phone call with Mom.

V.

I counted the minutes until my shift ended so that I could go and see him, and I was already imagining how after his friendly talk with Mom, he would greet me with a smile and invite me to sit down and ask how he could help. He would tell me that he understood and that he'd do everything he could to make things better for me. But that's not what happened.

That evening it started raining, the kind of hard rain you get only on military bases. I ran from the war room to the HQ and looked for him in his office, but he wasn't there. Two soldiers told me there'd been a terrorist attack and he'd gone to a meeting called by the brigade commander.

I have to honestly admit that I couldn't have cared less about any terrorist attack at the time. I—who since roughly the age of five had watched the news on TV almost every night, who was familiar with every economic plan, leader, state, war, and terrorist, who knew of every event that happened anywhere in the world, but particularly in Israel, who during attacks would sit for hours watching TV and listening to all the analyses and the interviews and the pundits predicting how Israel would react and discussing who had carried out the attack—I no longer took an interest in the reality occurring outside my pathetic, painful existence.

I sat down on a bench outside his office and waited. The rain falling on my head and face had no effect on me, nor did I care how ridiculous I looked to the soldiers walking by. I'd looked ridiculous in their eyes a long time before that, and the last thing I cared about that evening was repairing that image. When I first got to the base, I was the religious soldier who was always going to prayers. Then I was the one who kept crying to the commander, the one who kept asking questions, the one who cared about honesty and truth and made a point of correcting people's grammar, the one who read biographies of Heine and Yonatan Ratosh and asked anyone who said they liked music whether they liked Bob Dylan and Leonard Cohen, and if they said yes, something lit up in my eyes.

Yes, that's how I appeared to the people on that base. They also thought I was a shirker, because I tried to get out of things just as they did. They assumed I was "shafting" the other guys, because once I got sick leave when I was sick and I was supposed to stay for Shabbat, and even though in the end I did stay on the base, I got the reputation of someone who "shafts" everyone else.

I remember that Thursday. I really was sick. I had a fever and I was very congested. After a night without sleep, I went to the clinic adjacent to our barracks, and the doctor immediately gave me three days of sick leave and told me to rest at home. I remember the way the sergeant responded. There were so many lousy titles in that pathetic platoon, which had no more than ten soldiers but somehow needed a high-ranking lieutenant colonel to command it. So I guess it also needed a sergeant. And the sergeant said to me quietly, in a tone of voice that sounded like a Mafia threat, that in her opinion I should give up those sick leave days and not show them to Dan, because then he would have to let me go home, and that meant that someone else would have to give up their weekend instead of me.

I also remember how the guy who had to stay on base that weekend instead of me, who had presented himself as my friend, responded when he found out: he cursed me. I remember his black face and buggy eyes. I remember him coming to my room and letting out a stream of curses about how I was an asshole, and he'd get back at me, and I'd regret "shafting him," and I was ruining his life. "How am I ruining your life?" I asked. "Because," he said, "you're a son of a bitch."

I think about how that soldier came to our platoon from the infantry battalions because he dreamed of becoming an officer, but no one would let him be an officer in a combat unit. Now I remember that in the end they refused to make him an officer in Intelligence too, and I feel sorry for him. I feel sorry that his greatest dream was to control other people, to get respect from eighteen-year-old soldiers who were legally required to respect him because if they didn't they'd go to prison, and to walk around with his ranks on his shoulders and flash that grin of his, which exposed his big white teeth, and to tell anyone who would listen that he was an officer.

And no, I don't think I'm exaggerating at all, because I have no doubt that he didn't have a single good intention or ideal behind that dream of being an officer in the Israel Defense Forces, and it's a good thing for everyone who might have become his soldier that they wouldn't let him be an officer.

I don't know why I decided to stay on the base that weekend in the end, even though I had sick leave. I suppose my soul was so weak that I couldn't withstand the words and the looks and the curses. I think that Thursday was when my disgust with the army and with people in general, especially when they are people in the army, was at its height. I think that on that Thursday I understood, yet again, that all the talk about comradeship and friendship and trust in the army is meaningless nonsense.

VI.

After more than half an hour, he arrived. He looked the same as usual. The same walk, the same grin, the same disgust that comes up in me every time I remember him. Despite the rain and the freezing wind, his sleeves were rolled up above his elbows. He was holding a map I'd laminated earlier.

"Eli," I called out softly behind him, but he didn't hear. "Eli," I called again, and this time he turned to me with a cold, dry look. I expected him to know why I was addressing him, and that he would smile. But there was no smile.

"Um . . ." I stammered. "My mom talked with you and . . ." I scrutinized his face, hoping he'd remember his conversation with Mom that afternoon. "She said you told her I should come see you and we'd talk."

"I'm busy now," he said with an incisive, supremely confident voice, without a drop of courtesy.

"It's . . . It's important for me that I talk to you this evening," I said. I tried to say it confidently, but to my own ears it sounded like a whispered stutter. I remember his look of aversion, of unwillingness. A tired, derisive look. I remember his lips stretching into an expression that meant one thing: "I don't see what you and I could possibly have to talk about."

Playing innocent again. That is the verbal translation of what I felt when I heard that line come out of his mouth. I wanted to tell him that Mom had already talked to him, that she'd explained to him that I was . . . that I was having a hard time. And that I'd waited my whole shift to talk to him, hoping he could help me. Save me. Now in my room, I think what an idiot I was. How could he have helped me, that officer who seemed like God to me that day? Two stripes on his shoulder. A lieutenant colonel. He was also a junior officer, I realize now. He roamed the base like a stray dog looking for an ass to lick so that maybe he'd get a promotion, or just a kind word—an ego-stroke.

I remember one time when we were on that operation near Nablus, and the regimental commander needed a map urgently but it wasn't ready. I remember how Eli got annoyed and upset and raced back and forth, trying to please the commander on one end and yell at us on the other. I think about the madness I felt at that moment, which any normal person would have felt. I think about that grown man, whom some people even addressed as "General," racing back and forth across a span of twenty feet at most, one moment shouting furiously, threatening, sulking, and the next laughing, making jokes, putting his hand on the commander's shoulder, asking obsequious questions, then walking back again to shout and prod and threaten, then back again, twenty feet, laughing then turning serious and listening and flattering, and over and over again for several minutes.

I remember his sycophancy, the way he stuck to the regimental commander like a mollusk with his fleshy, droopy lips, wearing a tiny yarmulke that attested to nothing related to morality or truth, certainly not to God, with his gut—his potbelly—spilling over, and his small blue eyes. Then he punished us and we had to laminate all the maps, including the ones we'd already done. "I don't care," he said, "get all the plastic off and redo them."

VII.

"Wait for me in my office in half an hour," he said after he realized he wouldn't be able to get rid of me. I went to my room to have dinner. I preferred eating instant noodles in my room to sitting in the dining room, where I had to see the hypocrisy and stupidity of the other soldiers, the ones whom any ordinary, "normative," patriotic Israeli would call "my brothers," but who were, to me, mere rivals for furloughs and weekends off, for a better bed, for more rest, for holidays off, for making a better impression.

After a little less than half an hour I was back at his door. I remember the building where his office was housed. Our whole platoon was there. Three doors. The first was the lieutenant colonel's room, the second was a little room that contained both the second lieutenant Gali's office and a kitchenette where I drank coffee every morning. Or rather, at first I drank coffee there every morning with the other soldiers, but later I would sit in the synagogue and read Psalms and pray for everything to work out. And the third room was the workroom. That's where I went after prayers, and I'd wait quietly on an office chair for someone to tell me what to do.

How difficult that silence was for me. The compulsion to be quiet, the inability to put together a precise or witty sentence. In my "ordinary" life—my life from Thursday or Friday to Sunday, apart from once every four weeks—my primary skill was my ability to make people laugh, or to embarrass them. Without that, I was simply helpless.

I escaped into phone calls a lot. I would call Ayala or Michal or Dror. Sometimes I think I loved Ayala in that period only so that I could call her, so that I could feel that I was "someone." When she answered—or Michal, when I called her—I became different. I was funny and trenchant, although it didn't really matter what I was, as long as I could talk. It was only on those phone calls that I really talked. I remember Michal trying to encourage me the way she always did, in her ordinary, banal way, by saying "you have to," and "everyone gets through it," and "think about the future." When I asked who said I had to destroy myself because "everyone gets through it," and who said that everyone who "gets through it" feels the way I do, she would repeat the same things in different words, and the whole thing would start over again. To be honest, even today, when I'm no longer in touch with her, I remember those conversations fondly, because no matter what was said in them, no matter if they were smart things or terribly dumb things—and to me they were terribly dumb— the important thing was that I talked, that I made a voice and someone listened, and I felt as if I still existed, the way I wanted to exist: sharp, piercing, smart, funny.

Ayala kept telling me I should leave the army. I replay the conversation we had in my mom's car, when Ayala said she would always be with me, and that I didn't have to be afraid that no woman would want me if I got out of the army for mental health reasons, because she would be with me whatever happened. Now in my room, I think about her. About her high-pitched voice, her white skin, her ugly smile that was sometimes so beautiful, like that time she came back after a week in Eilat and I went to see her, and when she opened the door she smiled at me and I knew she'd missed me.

I think about her crying too. She told me that after the first time she cried because of me, her mother said that if she was crying that meant she'd lost. "Lost what?" I asked her, and maybe I felt good about what her mother had said. "I don't know," she said with a laugh and made a helpless motion with her hands, "The woman is nuts."

Then I remember her crazy streaks. I remember that once she was driving and she tried to kill us both, zigzagging like a madwoman and not letting me touch the wheel. "Get your hands off!" she screamed, and her eyes almost popped out. "This is my car!" Then she said, "Don't touch the wheel! That's the last time you're touching the wheel!" Eventually she came around and started crying. "I can't take it anymore," she said, "I feel like we're slowly dying."

VIII.

When I got to Eli's office, he was just walking out. "Wait here," he said and marched away arrogantly, self-importantly. I went in and sat down on one of the chairs scattered around the long conference table. Sometimes, I remember now, we would sit around that table listening to a lesson on the weekly Torah portion from the military rabbi whose office was nearby.

I was anxious. My feet tapped nervously on the floor and my palms were clammy. I felt that my future depended on what happened in that room. I silently recited verses from Psalms, which I knew by heart because I made a point of saying them every day after prayers. Then I looked around. I looked at the Israeli flag and the platoon flag that faced each other. I looked at the desk; it was full of papers, and among them was an empty paper cup with brown liquid residue stuck to its bottom. I looked at the little shelf above his desk chair. There were four books: a biography of some general who later became a government minister, two mass market novels, and one book of poetry. Every officer must have at least one poetry collection displayed over his head, I thought scathingly. Then I remembered that the first time I'd seen that book, it had made me happy, because I thought how wonderful it was that I had an officer who read poetry, and that he must be a man with a tender soul.

What an idiot I was back then, I thought to myself. I remembered one Tuesday when Eli said we would get the evening off as long as we completed a job he gave us, but when we finished he said he'd changed his mind and we weren't getting off. Apart from his nasty behavior, what I remember most from that evening was one of the soldiers. He had a large forehead and his red hair was combed up in something attempting to be a forelock but which looked like a crest. He fumed and cursed the lieutenant colonel, and said we should rebel or something, and we should boycott him and stop letting him pretend to be our friend and then screw us over. Even though we weren't friends, I felt close to that soldier at that moment, because I thought he was right, and also because I was very disappointed that we weren't going home. Later, after I showered and went back to the platoon room, I saw the same soldier joking around with the lieutenant colonel as if they were great pals, as if he hadn't acted like a louse by leaving us on the base for no reason. I remember him, that goddamn redhead, prancing around Eli and telling him more and more jokes and kissing his baboon ass.

Scum, I thought to myself when I saw that. Miserable scum. What happened to all those things you said, which I believed you were saying honestly? What happened to the rebellion and the boycott, which I carried out? I really did boycott him: when I went to take a shower I walked past him without saying hello. I felt disgusted. And while I waited for him anxiously in his office that evening, bolting at every rustle I heard outside because I thought it might be him, I felt that same disgust. Then the disgust gave way to fear that perhaps I was the pathetic one in this scenario. Perhaps it was me who was the inferior one, because I didn't know how to act in these places and how to handle people like him. Maybe I was the stupid one. Maybe I was too innocent. Even though I didn't usually consider myself naive.

He turned up after more than an hour and a half. When he walked in and I glared at him, I could feel my eyes exuding fear. He perfunctorily apologized for being late. Then he stretched his arms out, sank into the chair, and said, "Right, so how can I help you?"

Before I went to see him, when I was still on my shift in the war room, I'd promised myself I would be as honest with him as I could. I wouldn't hold back from crying or telling him exactly how I felt. I thought about that decision in that moment.

"Um . . ." I started awkwardly. His impatient face did not make things easier. Remember what you decided, I told myself over and over again. Remember those moments on the side of the road, standing there waiting for a car to pass so you can jump in front of it. Then I reminded myself of that night with Dror when I asked him to break my hand.

"I can't," Dror had said. "You have to," I told him, practically sobbing. "Hold the car door and slam it on my hand. As hard as you can." Dror said nothing. He couldn't understand how a person could ask someone to break his hand just to get a few days off.

"More than a month of sick leave!" I yelled at him. "Do you know what more than a month of sick leave means?" We were on the beach, and other than a few people sitting at one of the wooden tables, there was no one else there. "You promised me you'd do it!" I shouted. I remembered my own words, and him being quiet. I wanted to force him to do it, to make him injure me, to make him break my hand.

At first I'd asked him to break my foot. We were in the car, and I told him I thought the best thing to do was break a limb, because then you got a long leave. He sat there silently. The idea had been kicking around my mind for a long time, but the minute I said it, like a stubborn decision to hit on a girl, come what may, I got carried away and decided that whatever happened, I wanted him to break my foot. "We'll go to the beach," I said, "then you call my parents and tell them I fell or I accidentally shut the door on my foot and I can't drive, and I might have broken something and someone has to take me to the hospital." Then I added that I'd heard it was easier to get sick leave at the hospital in Nahariya than in Haifa, "So if I'm dying of pain and I can't talk, tell them I said to take me to Nahariya."

In the end he refused to break anything. "My blood is on your hands," I shouted at him furiously, like a madman.

"You're a coward. You're just a miserable, stinking, self-righteous coward. Don't you see how self-righteous you are? How can you study Torah with that self-righteousness? You're like all the other scum. Like all the other self-righteous scum."

Then I drove him home silently. He looked kind of sorry for himself, and I wanted to vomit on him. Then I wanted to cry. When he got out of the car I stayed outside his home, sitting in the car, staring at a spot on the road, and I didn't know what to do. It was a Saturday night, and I had to go back to the base the next day.

IX.

"This place is bad for me," I blurted after reminding myself about that day with Dror.

"What do you mean, bad for you?" he asked and squinted at me. "Are you being mistreated? Can you point to something or someone specific?"

"That's not it," I said, "I'm just unhappy here. I don't know, maybe it's the job, maybe it's . . ."

"Do you want to switch jobs?" he asked.

"I don't know. I mean . . ."

Then the conversation evolved into a dialogue between two deaf people, with me trying to scream out everything that was hurting and him screaming so he wouldn't have to hear. He told me I was spoiled, that he had bigger things to worry about, that "this is the army" and he wasn't supposed to "deal with kindergarten problems."

"It's not kindergarten problems," I said and almost burst into tears. "I'm really unhappy. I really can't be here. I feel like I'm going crazy. Once I even wanted to jump in front of a moving car so I could get sick leave . . ."

"What do you mean jump?"

I could see how he suddenly perked up and peered at me, as if the phrase "his eyes lit up" had been invented right then about him. But although I understood the meaning of his question and his newly alert gaze, I quickly downplayed the significance of the words I'd only just uttered, and said it was nothing, that I thought about it but I didn't do anything, but that he needed to understand what state I was in and what thoughts I was having, so that he'd help me. Like an idiot, I thought he could help me. I am overcome again by the heavy realization of how naive I was about the destructive system that is the army: How could I have thought that such a pathetic officer, a petty officer with no power over the system, could help me?

"I'd appreciate if you could give me furlough," I said finally, a moment before he stood up and said he had a lot of work, and practically kicked me out of the office, completely shattered.

"I don't know if I can give you furlough now," he said, and other than kicking me in the butt he did everything he could to make me leave his office so he could forget about me.

I remember the night that awaited me outside. I remember the stifling closeness of the black air, the sensation of missed chances, of defeat, of failure. In the end I walked out of that office just as lost as I'd been when I went in, without even a shred of hope to help me get through the next day and go home for Shabbat. I'd been anticipating some sort of salvation, but again there was nothing. Again I'd have to get up the next morning with the same people, again I'd have to sit in that rotten war room, laminating and cutting, over and over again.

I could feel the suffocation filling me completely and I didn't know what to do. I knew I had no chance, that I was completely powerless in the face of the system and the people who populated it, people who weren't interested in anything except their own asses and who didn't even have the most basic human capacity: the capacity to listen and try to help. I walked along the muddy paths, and at some point, next to a storeroom, I leaned against a big green trash can and started to cry. I ran images of the next morning through my mind, and of the next week, and the days that had passed and would yet pass, and the long prayers and the stomachaches and the meals alone in my room, and the miserable, tedious work, and the mornings in the bunk bed when my eyes opened to the niggling ring of the alarm clock that always penetrated my dreams and didn't stop ringing until the terrible understanding that there was no choice, I had to jump out of bed and quickly put on my filthy, baggy uniform, polish my boots, and stand for morning roll call full of dread because my boots might not be properly polished, or my beard, which I was allowed to keep because I was religious, might not have grown long enough since I'd shaved it on my weekend at home, and then to thank God that the master sergeant had run his eyes over my boots and my face without saying a word, and then the loneliness again.

I wanted to die. If there was ever a moment in my life when I genuinely wanted to die, when I honestly could have cocked my weapon and shot myself, it was then. I leaned against the big green trash can and stared at the storehouse and the road next to it. That's where I was when Dad called and asked how the talk went. "It sucked," I told him, and tears started streaming from my eyes again. "I don't know," I mumbled into the phone, "I don't know, I don't know, I don't know." I felt completely lost. What was there to be done at that point? What? Mom, throughout the whole story, with the whole disgusting mess of talks with the lieutenant colonel and the first lieutenant—and I keep having to write this over and over again—was as determined as a ball of fire. She was a lioness. She said she was calling him right then and that I should hang tight and not do anything.

"I want to die," I told them for the first time. "I want to die. I just want to die," I said, like a man who has lost his last remaining hope. I was no longer afraid to worry or sadden them. I realized I had no choice. That if I didn't tell them how I was really feeling, they would understand only after it happened.

X.

Mom told me later that she'd called the commander and told him she wanted to come and take me home; she didn't want to get me back in a body bag and then have them tell her how sorry they were and how they didn't know how such a thing could have happened. I don't know what else she told him. I only know that after a while a soldier turned up, a guy I hated and who hated me, and he said that Eli had woken him up and told him to take away my weapon so I wouldn't put a bullet through my head.

How despicable can a person be? I thought to myself as I took my rifle off and handed it to the soldier. How despicable, to wake a soldier up in the middle of the night so he could take away my weapon just to humiliate me. That's what I thought and that's what I still think. Because why couldn't Eli himself—the lieutenant colonel, with his two stripes, that fat slob who reeked of self-importance—why couldn't he have come to find me by the green trash can and taken my weapon himself, instead of going to wake up that soldier? He wasn't even capable of doing that bare minimum.

"They took my weapon away," I told Dror on the phone when I was on the way to the synagogue to pick up my tefillin, which I kept under the prayer shawls in the cabinet beneath the holy ark. "Those dogs want to humiliate me. They think this is how they're going to humiliate me."

I shouted those words at Dror, and then I cried. I told him what had happened with Eli. He was the only one I called. I couldn't take Michal's encouraging words, or that loving, disgusting, stupid, tender voice of Ayala's. In the synagogue I read Psalms for an hour, maybe more, until Mom and Dad called and said they were at the gate.

Mom hugged me and I couldn't stop crying. After a while I calmed down and looked out the car window. I pictured myself as a little boy, and I remembered how I used to like driving at night when we came back from a trip or a family event. Then I remembered that once I was coming back from a wedding with Dad and we listened to an old Israeli folk song called "The Lady in Brown." I sang that song quietly to myself.

Dad was wearing a blue tracksuit and Mom was in house clothes. Dad drove with a sort of determination and hardly spoke. I knew he was disappointed. I didn't know how to placate him except to try to explain what I was feeling.

"But I can't understand it," he said when I tried once again to explain what I was going through.

"What can't you understand?" I screamed. "What can't you understand? It's a fact, I want to die, I want to die now, today, if you hadn't come I'd be dead. I'd be dead! Can you understand *that*?"

My whole body was shaking and I couldn't steady my breath. We were close to home by then and I felt as if I were suffocating. Mom kept saying, "Stop, enough. Calm down.

Enough. Here, see, we're going home." When Dad repeated that he couldn't understand and he didn't know why I felt that way or how he could help, and that all he knew was that everyone got though it and even if it was a little rough then you got over it, Mom told him to stop already and be quiet and that this wasn't the time for all those lines.

We walked inside silently. When I lay on the bed I didn't feel anything. For the first time in ages, I was calm. "I'm not going back there," I'd said when we got out of the car and went inside, and that statement had calmed me. For one single moment I believed I could avoid going back to the army, that I could be saved from the decree I was committed to by law, from that thing that was dragging me into the abyss.

CHAPTER THREE

I.

_____

The journey to the mental health clinic grew slower and slower. As we got closer to the center of the country and the morning wore on, there were more and more vehicles on the road, and the air filled with dirt and a stifling sensation. Dad sipped the coffee he'd bought half an hour earlier at a gas station and looked at me.

"These drives," he said, "they remind me of our trip in the U.S."

"Yes," I answered, "except the circumstances were different."

"True," he answered hesitantly, and I knew he was bringing up that trip just to somehow break the tension. Then he said nothing, just crawled along in the line of cars moving heavily, each to its own destination.

"Look at all these people," he said and gestured at the cars around us in the traffic jam. "Look at them. Ninety percent of them were in the army."

"I know that, Dad," I said, "but what does that have to do with me?"

"I'm just saying," he said, playing innocent. "It just drives me crazy to see you suffering, and I can't understand it."

"I hope they help me at this MHO," I said.

Dad said nothing for a while, and then he said, "To tell you the truth, I'm not sure how they can help you. Even if they do, let's say they move you to a different base, maybe even to one nearby where you can come home every day, I still don't know how much that's really helping."

"What do you mean?" I asked.

"I'm not sure that the loss won't outweigh the gain, you see?" He was talking about his fear that they'd give me a low mental health profile and I'd be considered mentally ill.

"I don't think there's another solution," I said. "I mean, I know there's no other solution."

Then he repeated that maybe I needed to try harder, and I got angry again and said this had nothing to do with trying and that I was sick of saying the same things over and over again. He offered to talk to someone he knew, who might be able to help me without going through this whole MHO thing, and I knew how hard it was for him to ask for help, especially when he'd have to tell someone that his son had mental health issues, and worse—that his son couldn't cope with the army, which every loser gets through without any trouble.

"But Dad," I said wearily, looking at the face of the driver sitting in the car next to us, "we've already tried talking to someone you know, haven't we? It doesn't work, all those talks."

"Yes, but maybe this time . . ." he started to say, but he realized I was right, so he stopped talking.

II.

I remembered the last time he tried to get help, from a member of our synagogue whose son was friendly with the commander of the base where I was serving. That was after the furlough I got as a result of that night when I talked with the lieutenant colonel and said I was thinking about dying, and he woke up that pathetic soldier to come and take my gun, and Mom and Dad came to pick me up, and Dad told me again that he couldn't understand it, and that I had to try harder and not give in so easily.

I almost had a nervous breakdown then, and when Sunday came around and I had to go back, I told Mom and Dad that I wasn't going, and I just stayed in bed and cried endlessly. In the end they broke down, called the commander and convinced him to extend my furlough. But after it ended, after I kept telling myself that I wasn't going back to the army anymore, and I stupidly thought I could get out of it, I found myself on the base again, and this time I was almost alone there, because everyone else was on the other base for some operation. They arranged for me to stay on the base without doing much of anything, just hand out maps from the "map warehouse" to anyone who came to ask for one.

It was horrible. I felt trapped inside myself, wandering around an abandoned base all day. In the daytime I watched Channel One, the only channel the antenna picked up on the TV in the workroom, and I slept a lot. After being in that state for a week, then going home for the weekend and having to go back to the base yet again on Sunday, Dad told me he'd talked to someone from our synagogue who would arrange for me to get help from the base commander within a few days. But meanwhile, he said, I shouldn't cause problems, because otherwise everything would fall apart and the commander wouldn't help me.

And indeed, after two days during which I did nothing except give one map to someone who'd come especially from the other base, and another time when the first lieutenant, Dan, suddenly turned up and didn't like the fact that I wasn't doing anything so he told me to clean the map warehouse, the son of the man from our synagogue called me.

I remember his saccharine voice when he told me that my base commander had talked to him, and that starting tomorrow I'd be an "HQ soldier." He said I should wait for the commander the next morning outside his office, and that he would see what he could do with me. I think about that sentence: "what he could do with me." As if I was a thorn that had to be pulled out of someone's foot. Or an infected wound that had to be lanced so the pus would come out.

The next morning I waited for the commander by his office, but he went in and then came out without looking at me. Around midday I plucked up the courage, and when he walked out of the office again I explained who I was and asked when I could come in. He barely looked at me, just said I had to wait outside until he called me. I waited until evening, when he sent a soldier out to tell me I could go to sleep and come back the next day. That's what happened the next day too. On the third day, he suddenly called me in and asked how he could help.

I remember that he used the same puffed-up, self-important tone I already knew from the other commanders. The same weariness and impatience, as if he couldn't care less about me. The same feigned innocence that characterized everyone who'd interviewed me up till then, the same revulsion at this broken vessel sitting before him, the person who'd waited for three days to talk to him, to this base commander who couldn't even speak correct Hebrew, who'd never read a book or listened to classical music, who had nothing new to tell me about life or emotions or truth, who had nothing except the loathsome and unjust capacity to determine my future. To decide whether I would live or die.

"You're not getting a day job with me," he said decisively when I asked if I could go home every day. "This isn't a base for cunts," he explained, "and if you don't have a reason why you need to leave every day, you stay here like everyone else. And you do guard duty like everyone else and you do kitchen duty like everyone else. Got it?"

"But I do have a reason!" I suddenly said with a confidence I hadn't been aware of.

"What's the reason?" he asked, and a smile of contempt spread over his face. He lit a cigarette.

"The reason is the same reason why I'm here. The reason is that I just can't do it, mentally. That I'm unhappy."

"You're unhappy?" he said derisively. "You're unhappy? Do you have some sort of confirmation from a doctor or an MHO or a shrink that you're . . . unhappy?"

I wished I could tell him that if I'd wanted to go to the MHO and get an authorization, I wouldn't have waited for him outside for three days, and that if I had an MHO's authorization I'd have shown it to him straight away and gone home. Then I wanted to ask why he was being sanctimonious, why he was conveniently forgetting that he'd talked to the son of the guy from my synagogue, who'd told him the whole story, and that he'd promised to help me, and that was why he'd moved me to the HQ that he was in charge of. But instead of all those confident, solid words, the only thing that came out was a weak, muffled, "Do you want me to get authorization from the MHO?"

I hoped he'd tell me to go to the MHO. I hoped he'd say he couldn't help me, that only the MHO could. I hoped he'd say that so that I could tell Dad that even this violent man with the green eyes, the commander of the base, who acted as if he were omnipotent, who had the mediocre Hebrew of someone off the street, who in three years would be completely bald—that even he'd told me to see the MHO. I wanted to be done with this saga of asking people for help. I already knew that nothing was going to come of this commander either, and that without going to the MHO and getting a binding, official letter, it was all just a show of power and respect that each one of these people, these adults with their stripes, was doing on my back.

"I don't recommend seeing the MHO," he answered drily. "I don't recommend that anyone do that. But if you say you're unhappy and you think you *must* be at home every day"—he mimicked my voice when he said that—"if that's the case, then yes, you need to go to the MHO so he can give you an authorization that says you need to sleep every night in your own bed in your own room with your teddy bear or your whatever. Either way, I can't help you."

III.

After that talk, I told Dad what the commander had said and he simply refused to believe it. He asked me to repeat his precise words several times. Because Dad was fighting the idea of me going to the MHO since he was terrified of the repercussions of a mental health exemption.

"You have to understand," he kept saying, "you have to understand that in any case going to the MHO is not such a simple matter. I know you can't see it now, but I know enough cases of people who had some problem in the army, and they thought the simplest thing would be to go to the MHO and ask for a mental health allowance, or a complete exemption, and after they did that and got what they wanted, they really were happy for a while, but now, in all sorts of respects, their lives are much more difficult. I'm telling you, I know these stories firsthand."

"What do you mean, in all sorts of respects?" I asked him.

"In all sorts of respect means, first of all, in terms of work. You know that any potential employer, the first thing he'll do, before anything else, is have you sign a confidentiality waiver and pull your medical records? Just imagine—what employer is going to hire a person with a mental health exemption to work for him?" Then he said, "Also, in terms of finding a wife, it's not that simple. Let's say that the woman herself won't have a problem with it, because she'll know you and she'll know you're totally fine. But think for a moment about her parents. What parents would want their daughter to marry someone who has mental health issues? Think about it: What are you going to tell them when you spend Shabbat at their house and the father asks you what you did in the army?"

I sat silently for a few moments. The things Dad said frightened me. I didn't want to ruin my life. But did I have a choice? I wondered. And I realized I didn't. I couldn't see any other option.

"It's better to live with difficulties than to die, isn't it?" I said slowly.

"Right now you want to die and not cope with the difficulties," he answered quickly, using his ability to turn things upside down.

"It's not that," I said, "there's a solution here. Why should a person suffer this much, suffer so much that he wants to die, if there's a solution to his problem?"

"It's not a solution. Don't you understand?" he said, and I realized again how hard it was for him to accept that I would go to the MHO and have a mental health record. I remembered all the times he used to drive me to the base, more than an hour each way, and sometimes he'd wait there for whole days so I'd feel safe. Just like a parent who takes his child to kindergarten and doesn't leave until the child stops crying, I think now. He used to call me a few times a day to ask if everything was all right, and when I had to stay for Shabbat he would bring me food.

There's no doubt that Dad tried every solution he could think of, until that night, the night when I banged my head against the wall more than fifty times, the night when the three of us cried, him and Mom and I. He must have been filled with despair or a sense that there was nothing left to do. I remember him coming to my room at quarter to five in the morning to see if I'd fallen asleep, and finding me lying awake in bed, humming to myself.

"Why aren't you asleep?" he asked.

"I can't sleep. I can't stop thinking."

"But you have to sleep."

I didn't answer. He didn't say anything either. I stared at the ceiling.

"Do you want to go to the MHO?" he asked suddenly, and I could see the despair in his eyes mingling with tiredness and puffiness from crying. "Do you really feel that's the solution?"

I didn't answer. I kept looking up at the ceiling. Then I said I thought we'd tried everything else.

"If you want to, then let's go. Get up and we'll leave. You have to get there before eight, don't you?"

IV.

I'm a lefty. I have to be a lefty. When that thought got stuck in my head, I asked myself: Have you ever been a soldier in the Occupied Territories? Do you even know what it means to stand in the sun for eight hours checking people who are trying to get from one place to another? Do you know what it means to feel the sweat dripping down your whole body? And to smell their sweat? And every single day to see those faces that hate you? And to be afraid that at any minute someone might blow your head off? You know they want to destroy us, don't you?

No. I've never been a soldier in the territories. I haven't stood in the sun for eight hours, except on school trips. And I know everyone wants to destroy us. Ever since I was a kid I've known everyone wants to destroy us. But I have to be a lefty.

"Why?" Dad asked when I told him.

"Why?" I laughed bitterly, "Why? Because I'm under military rule myself, don't you see? Just like the Palestinians. I too get told when to go and when to come and what to eat and how I'm allowed to talk. I too get punished on a whim and screamed at on a whim and treated nicely on a whim, and on agendas and on questions of honor. And sometimes they let me suffer and they treat me indifferently, cruelly, just to teach me what military discipline is and what being a soldier is. And if that's what they're capable of doing to me, when I'm supposedly 'one of them,' their own soldier, someone who doesn't want to destroy anyone, certainly not them, a soldier who only wanted to contribute what he could and get through his three years, then just think what they're capable of doing to the Palestinians, whom they define as their enemy. Think!"

"You keep saying 'them, theirs,'" Dad said, evading the political issue, "as if it's not you, not us. As if you don't belong to it."

"I say 'them, theirs,' precisely because it's me, us," I said. "I say that because these people who are supposed to treat me like one of their own treat me like I'm their enemy, don't you understand? Because they hate me too. I say 'them' because I just can't stand this feeling that the entity that represents me, that is supposed to be my operational branch as a citizen of this country, as a human being, is exactly that entity— the army. And even worse, that this entity, which can legally demand that I be willing to die for it, is the entity that's causing me all this suffering. Don't you understand?"

V.

I remember the day I went to ask the first lieutenant for an authorization to see the MHO. He had to complete a form called "Commander's Affidavit," which stated that I was depressed, not useful, crazy. Without that form, no soldier can see the MHO.

It was on the base near Nablus. They were there again on some operation that occurred after a terrorist attack. In those days there was an attack almost every day, but I had no connection with that reality of terrorism. It was the first time in my life when I didn't follow the news and didn't know what was going on in the country, and to be honest it didn't interest me. My pain removed me from the overall reality. I was no longer part of it, of that "us."

I remember Dan, the first lieutenant, walking out of the tent that served as a mess hall. It was a hot day, and Dad had driven me to the base just to get the form, so that if I eventually wanted to go to the MHO we'd be able to go. That was after my talk with the base commander, who told me that if I wanted to get any kind of exemption I had to get authorization from the MHO. Dan—who was only a first lieutenant—walked out of the big tent, and for a moment he looked like Napoleon. His epaulettes looked as if they were raised up off his shoulders, as if he had shoulder pads. His hair was brown and dense and it was getting long. He had slightly slanted eyes. Light-colored. I couldn't deal with him. I remember the look in his eyes when he saw me waiting for him: he looked as if he were cursing me.

When I saw him walking out and looking at me like that, I remembered the first time I'd seen him. It was when I got to the platoon and he interviewed me. I remembered his confident talk, as if we were at a debriefing for a military operation or about to conquer a house or a city.

"We're looking for serious soldiers here," he said, "soldiers who work and don't mess around. Do you understand? I'm not interested in sob stories about your girlfriend who dumped you last week, or your dog who put a bullet through his head. What I need is work, period. Sunday through Thursday or Friday. Plus one weekend a month. Do you think you're that kind of soldier? Can you handle that?"

"Yes, sure," I answered immediately, to impress him, and then I added that I'd come to this platoon because it was where soldiers could make the greatest contribution, and if I couldn't be in combat because of the asthma, at least I would be in a home front unit that made the biggest contribution.

When I think back to his disdain in that intake interview, I don't think he believed all my lofty talk. And not because it was me, but because he already knew that all those words don't last more than two weeks in that defective system called the army.

I also remembered the talk he had with me after Mom called him a few days after I broke down on the phone. It was at the end of the operation, the first one I took part in, after we'd come back to our home base. He was nice, maybe even more than that. He spoke to me candidly. We were in his room, and we each sat on a bunk bed.

"Look," he said, "I don't really know how I can help you. I mean, you know how it works in the army, you have to get authorizations for everything, and . . ." It wasn't his words that gave me a good feeling when I left his room, and made me call Mom and tell her I thought things were going to be all right. It was the way he said them, the honesty, without any talk of ideals. He lay on his bed with his shirt unbuttoned, smoking a cigarette. I also remember fondly how he offered me some Coke from the half-empty bottle next to his bed. Not that Coke was such a rare commodity or that I particularly like it, it's just that since then, in all the talks I've had with people, no one has ever offered me a Coke or anything else to drink.

VI.

"I came for the MHO authorization," I said.

"Did you bring the form?" he asked impatiently.

"Yes," I answered, and I remembered all the times I'd felt affection toward him, when he was in a good mood and he would come into the workroom or sit down on the bench and talk with the other soldiers and me. I remembered that once I found a note he'd written to his girlfriend. He wrote that he loved her, that he wanted her to love him, that he was scared of being without her. He was scared of being alone and he felt things weren't going as well as they used to.

Then I remembered that time when he told me he'd rather be in Intelligence than in army radio or somewhere were you did nothing, and that if he could he would continue to be a combatant. I couldn't understand his admiration of the army, and I asked him a few times whether he was serious, and he looked at me and said he couldn't understand why I was so surprised. Now I think that maybe in his case the admiration of the army was genuine. Maybe at the end of the day he really was a naive kibbutznik who thinks the army is everything. And maybe that's why he didn't go on about ideals. Because for him it was real, not just empty words.

"Okay," he said when I handed him the paper, "wait here. I'll fill it out." He went back into the tent he'd just left. After a few minutes he came out and asked if I had a pen.

"Yes," I said and tossed him a pen, and he went back in.

I leaned against the concrete wall opposite the mess hall tent. It was on the second base, the one where I'd broken down on the phone with Mom and Dad for the first time, and cried the way I hadn't cried for years when Mom asked how I felt and I could no longer say that everything was okay. I looked around at the base. I looked at the ice-cream machine next to me, outside the war room, rattling like a refrigerator. I remembered how every night when I was on shift I would buy a strawberry ice cream, and I would sit down on the cement wall I was leaning on now, and I would lick it slowly, to kill time.

Sometimes Ayala would call me on those nights. I remembered one time when she called after we hadn't been in touch for a long time. She sounded sleepy and said she just wanted to tell me she loved me. I wanted to tell her that she kept disappearing and then she'd suddenly call and say she loved me or ask if I'd marry her, and that it was nuts and she had to decide if we were together or not, because sometimes it really drove me crazy and I couldn't make sense of it in my mind. But instead I kept quiet and let her words, her hoarse voice, hoarse from tiredness and maybe from pain, fill me up, and I shut my eyes and felt the rhythm of my heartbeat, which sped up every time she said those words to me. To be honest, in those times, there, near Nablus, within the great loneliness I felt, those phone calls were my salvation. Them—and the synagogue.

Afterward I watched the soldiers walking in and out of the war room. Some of them I knew, others I didn't. I hadn't been with the unit for more than a month. After I crashed, and the lieutenant colonel took my gun and agreed that my parents could come and take me home and then agreed to give me furlough, I went back to my regular base, which as far as my platoon was concerned had been completely abandoned. That was thanks to intervention by the son of the guy from synagogue, and once I was there I kept getting more and more sick leave. I spent most of my sick leave days in bed, afraid to think about the day when I would have to go back. Sometimes I managed to suppress the pain for a few hours, but most of the time it was with me.

Some of the people I knew looked at me like I was a nutcase. Apparently after that night, when Lieutenant Colonel Eli woke up that dirty soldier and told him to take my gun away, he told everyone that I'd lost my mind. "Chin up," one soldier said as he walked by and slapped my shoulder. I wanted to throw up in his face. I wanted to shout at him that I was fine. Completely fine. I wanted to ask him if the fact that I couldn't get along in the army meant that there was something wrong with me. If the fact that I couldn't get along in a system whose entire essence was honor and power and authority, and more honor and more power and more authority, meant that I was crazy. But I didn't say anything. I just nodded like I knew things would be okay.

I looked at how pathetic they were, those soldiers who, unlike me, were supposedly "fine." It was a kingdom of slaves, I thought. They walked around hunched, wearing uniforms like prisoners' outfits. Their noses looked long and their eyes were red. Like ants. I swear. So pathetic, repressed, lacking selfhood, lacking the true ease felt by a man who sits in a cafe looking at a woman, or a man who laughs wholeheartedly at a good joke, out of happiness.

Then I remembered all the times they used to send me to the master sergeant, to be his gofer. I remembered mornings after roll call, when I'd turn up at the shipping container where all his equipment was, and he'd wave a roll of trash bags at me, which meant I had to go around the base picking up everyone's trash. It was horrible. I remember the humiliation of walking among the soldiers, bending over to pick up Popsicle wrappers or cigarette butts or soda cans. It's a lousy feeling that stays forever, I think now, right inside a person's bones. I remembered myself walking among the laughing soldiers and asking them to move aside so I could pick up the trash they threw on the floor. So pathetic, wearing a ripped uniform with a fleece jacket that the platoon gave out when winter came, dragging an orange trash bag behind me. I remembered how sometimes, when it rained, I would slip and my pants would get muddy, and I couldn't even shower properly to get the dirt off because there were so many of us sharing one shower, and by the time I got there it was all filthy from hair and mud.

Then I turned to look back at the synagogue. A small, messy room with a holy ark by the wall. I got up and walked in that direction. For a few moments I stood in the doorway. I looked at the prayer books piled in a cabinet that looked like it might topple over any minute. Then I looked at an unbound pair of tefillin sitting on the ark. The leather straps dangled out of the box like two nooses. I felt a calmness begin to fill me, the way it did back then, when I used to go there to pray and sit for hours, thinking and fantasizing and imagining. Sometimes I would just go in for no reason, sometimes even in the middle of the night when I was on guard duty or couldn't fall asleep. I would turn on the light and look at the walls. Sometimes I would lean my head on one of the tables and cry. Silently. People who walked in thought I was asleep. Some would leave quietly, so as not to wake me, and others would curse me and all the religious soldiers and say that instead of helping other soldiers I always made up some nonsense about how I had to pray when in fact I was going to sleep and "shafting" everyone.

VII.

I remember that once someone came into the synagogue, the one on our regular base, and when he saw me there he let out a curse. I can't remember whether he cursed me or all religious people. I looked up and he saw that my eyes were red and puffy from crying, and he just walked out silently. Throughout that awful period in Intelligence, the synagogue was my hiding place, my refuge, my fortress. The place where I could escape or return to. The place where I could sit quietly and look at the wall, or sing to myself, or talk to myself, because who else did I have to talk to? For me the synagogue was like a terminal, a neutral place where no one could touch me no matter what happened. Outside they could destroy me. They could judge me for no good reason, they could throw me into prison just like that, they could ground me on the base for more than a month, they could laugh at me and curse me and scorn me. But all that was only on the outside. Inside the synagogue, I felt protected. Inside that terminal between the worlds I felt as if I could resume being an ordinary person. The way I did on weekends, from Thursday night or Friday through Sunday, when I went to synagogue with Dad and we talked about the situation in the territories and the corruption and about how something fundamental had to change in this country, otherwise the whole thing would go to hell and all the people who dreamed of a

Greater Israel could keep on dreaming while they begged for a visa to get into some other country. We talked about other things too and after we came home the whole family would eat dinner together, and Mom's food was delicious and it wasn't swimming in oil and it didn't give me indigestion or heartburn. Then I would meet Dror and we'd walk around for hours, talking, or I'd go out for a drink with Ayala. At first, when I'd only arrived on the base after leaving the combat boot camp because of the asthma that no one believed I had, I could lose myself in fantasies about my "ordinary" life at night too without anyone disturbing me. But that didn't last long because of all the operations and guard duties and missions, and then all I had left was three daily prayers in the synagogue. A creaky chair in the corner of a little room crowded with prayer books arranged on the shelf like a heap of bodies, and various other moth-eaten books that people had donated and that were lying around the synagogue gathering dust.

VIII.

It was in the army that I found God. I write "found" because I can't say that I discovered Him there: I was religious before joining the army, I went to religious schools, I was part of Israel's religious life, I was in a religious youth movement and I wore a yarmulke and I put on tefillin every morning, and there were even times when I was part of "the religious dream," the one that speaks of a Greater Israel and flattens out all the other values that Judaism offers. But despite everything my upbringing had instilled in me, one could say that I only found God in the army. There, of all places, among the dirt and the hypocrisy and the human foulness He created, I found Him. I found Him putting His hand on my shoulder when I cried, or playing music for me or singing me a lullaby when my soul was shattered. Those were the moments when I would shut my eyes and float off to other places, other lives, sometimes my own life on the outside, my "ordinary" life, and sometimes completely different ones. Sometimes I would stand on high stages or mountains. Sometimes I would sit on a chair while a pianist sat opposite me, playing only for me. Sometimes I would laugh while I floated. Sometimes I would cry. I had someone to talk to. I could talk to Him. Simply to Him.

Once, when Dror and I sat on a park bench near my house talking about God and what God was, I told him I had no idea what God was or where He existed, and that all I knew was that I loved Him, that I felt love for Him. When I write *love* I mean real love, in its purest sense, the way a man sees a tree and knows that it's a tree, and even though countless philosophers can prove to him that he can't really know it's a tree, he will still eventually hold out his arms and say that it is a tree. That is how I love God. I remember standing in the middle of the park, tired because it was late, yelling at the top of my lungs: "God, I love you! I love you!" And there was nothing in it beyond the simple emotion of love that filled me.

I know it sounds strange to feel love for something you can't see or hold in your hands, but that's how I felt. That's how I still feel. I remember that night again, when they took my gun away and I went to the synagogue to wait for Mom and Dad. I remember the tranquility I felt there, among the pews in front of the holy ark. I remember feeling as if someone were putting his hand on my shoulder and telling me everything would be okay. "But how will it be okay?" I shouted silently, wordlessly. I felt the hand on my shoulder again. I felt the tranquility again.

IX.

I sat there lost in thought about that army base, which had treated me kindly—with or without double quotes—and then broke me down once and for all, and after a few minutes he came out of the tent: a bushy-haired, slant-eyed Napoleon, a first lieutenant in the Israel Defense Forces, carrying two coffins on each of his shoulders.

"Why are you looking so sloppy?" he asked, glaring at my worn red boots. "When was the last time you polished those?"

After a pause, I told him I would polish them as soon as I got home. Then I said my father was waiting outside in the car, and I asked if I could have the form.

"Your dad is waiting outside?" I remember his voice stretching out into a thin drawl. "Who said you were going home now?"

"I'm planning to see the MHO tomorrow morning," I replied, and I felt the enervation taking over again. I didn't have any strength left for this performance, for this show of power, for this need to keep insisting that I had to get authorization for every single thing, even for this thing that was so obvious, because even if I'd wanted to I couldn't have gone back to the home base that day, and I certainly couldn't have stayed on the base near Nablus, because I had to get to the mental health services at Tel Hashomer by eight a.m., and if I'd slept on the base there was no chance I'd make it. I didn't have the strength for the stern expression, the furrowed brow, the authoritative voice, as if the two of us were standing on a stage.

"What if I was going to give you a job before you go home?" he said impatiently, and I had the feeling that he couldn't be bothered with the act either, but he was unable to break the habit, the pattern he'd learned over all his military years.

"It's after twelve and if I left now, then . . . "

"To tell you the truth," he cut me off in a cold, pained voice, "you're playing dumb, and it's really getting on my nerves."

Then he said that fortunately for me I was out of the platoon anyway, because otherwise he'd show me "what military discipline is." What *is* military discipline? I asked myself as I walked to Dad's car, parked in a dusty lot outside the base. I concluded that military discipline was first of all being an idiot, erasing yourself, your name, your moods, your emotions, your ability to feel things, your capacity to choose between love and hate, between faith and heresy, between truth and lies.

There are no truth and lies in the army. Truth is what the commander tells you, even though a moment before he said the exact opposite, and love is only what you feel for someone who is useful to you and only as long as he's useful to you. After that you can, and perhaps should, shit all over him. There's no right or wrong either. There's only military discipline—that clean, sterile, "logical" title that projects such calm, such truth. So stuck in our bloodstream, in our modes of thinking.

Then I thought that if that was the meaning of the term, if "military discipline" meant that I had to erase myself, my thoughts, my emotions—then I'd rather be a traitor than obey it. I stood looking at the giant cement walls I would never see again, and I realized that my miserable military service attested to the fact that, if truth be told, I'd never been willing to make that sacrifice.

X.

We were near the entrance to Tel Hashomer when we asked a soldier walking on the sidewalk where exactly the mental health services were. He told us to take the second entrance, then drive a few minutes farther through a manicured neighborhood of private residences.

Mom had called just before. She said she was leaving for work soon, and she just wanted to make sure everything was okay. She asked Dad how he'd managed with the drive and if we'd had something to eat, then she asked me if everything was all right, and told me that with God's help things would work out and that I had to believe that, I had to know there was no shame in going to the MHO, that everyone did it these days, certainly people who'd been through a lot less than I had, and that she knew I'd done everything I could and if I'd decided to go, if we'd decided to go, then we had to do it wholeheartedly.

Dad, who was still apprehensive about the MHO business, became impatient with Mom and finished the call. He wished her a good day and said they'd talk later. I knew he didn't want to turn this MHO thing into an ideal, into something one should do.

I remembered my parent-teacher conferences in high school. I remembered how Dad's face used to radiate disappointment when he heard something bad. He would always sit there quietly and listen to the teachers, and when we left he would walk beside me silently. I also remembered how on the way home, after I gave him my excuses, he would always end up saying: "The most important thing is your health."

Then I remembered that once I asked him why he didn't get angry with me. I said that the father of a good friend of mine told my friend that if he didn't take his studies seriously he could forget about any money, that if he had to retake his matriculation exams after the army he could forget about getting any money for that, and that he'd better start saving now because it cost a lot of money. "Why don't you say something like that to me?" I asked, wanting him, for once, to be angry instead of disappointed. I had the feeling that if he shouted at me for a change, I'd have a much easier time dealing with the anger than with the disappointment.

"I don't say things like that to you because it's a stupid thing to say," he replied. "I could easily tell you that, but then what? What's going to happen when you really do want to improve your grades? Am I not going to help you? Will you go out and get a job? Miss a year of college? Where's the sense in that? Besides, you know that with me there's no such thing as my money or your money. My money belongs to all of you kids. I mean, what am I working for? So that we'll be comfortable. Me and all of you."

I didn't say anything. What could I say to such a reasonable answer, an answer full of honesty and genuine love from a father to his son? Then he said he hoped I would realize on my own that school was important, and that he didn't believe in teaching through threats.

I looked at him in the car. We'd already driven through the entrance, and he was looking for parking. He looked tired. The bags under his eyes were puffy and little wrinkles were visible on his face. I remembered the night before, with his sobs and his broken voice. "What do you want me to do?" he'd asked me, his body tilting forward. "Tell me what you want."

I remembered my silence. My fear of deciding to go to the MHO. My fear of disappointing him, seeing his eyes extinguished. His lips trembling. Just the way they did later, at five a.m., after I'd lain awake in bed staring at the wall and humming songs to myself, unable to sleep. "Do you want to go?" he'd asked, and I knew this time he meant it.

"I don't think we have a choice," I replied. "We've tried everything, haven't we?"

"I don't know if we've tried everything," he said, perhaps still trying to salvage something after all. "But if you think it's what you need, then get up and put your clothes on. We have to get there before eight, don't we?"

And we left.

CHAPTER FOUR

I.

At the entrance to the chief medical officer's headquarters, all the emotions of the preceding period mingled inside me. I felt my heart pounding and my stomach churning. I thought about Ayala. I remembered again that she'd called me the night before and I hadn't answered. I remembered how I lay in bed while the phone rang and tried to keep thinking, robotically, about how I could get out of going back to the base the next morning even though I had no more sick leave. I remembered that I saw her name flashing on the screen and was overcome by a strong feeling of disgust.

Then I remembered that a few days before, she'd wanted to meet. I avoided her and said I couldn't, but she called after midnight and asked me to come outside, and when I did I saw her sitting with her back against the wall along the path to my house, crying. I wanted to throw up. I suddenly realized how that whole period of heartache and constant sorrow had turned me into a walking corpse, so much so that I couldn't contain anything except my own dying soul. Not even Ayala.

Then I remembered that a little over a week ago, Dad took me to a play so I could calm down a little. I sat in the theater, and even though I could see the actors moving and talking, and even though I understood what they were saying, none of it managed to break through to me, to that death sitting inside me like a stinking lump of shit, reeking like a rotting carcass—the death that must have positioned itself in me when I stood on the side of the road night after night, waiting for headlights to appear in the distance so I could jump, or when I looked at Dror wide-eyed and shouted at him to stop being self-righteous and cowardly and break my hand already. "Shut that lousy door on my hand already!"

I heard someone's cell phone ring, and the sound threw me out of my thoughts and back to the gate, which was painted brown, and to the thick trees planted around it. I remember the sign that said "Mental Health." I remember the large letters and the arrow pointing right. I remember Dad standing there, his body limp with exhaustion, mental or physical, also staring at the sign. His eyes were glazed, as if he couldn't understand what he was reading. Or perhaps he couldn't believe those words that looked so estranged, so unsympathetic to my plight—or to his.

Then I remember standing with my head bowed, looking at the sidewalk. "Why aren't you going in?" Dad asked. With my stomach still churning, I said I didn't know. I remember that he took a little step toward me and put his hand on my shoulder.

"There's no point debating it now," he said, "you wanted to come. You said you thought this was the only place they could help you. Go in, tell them what you're feeling, what you're struggling with, and I hope they really do understand and can help you."

"I didn't say they could definitely help me," I answered quietly and looked up. "What I said was that if there's a single place in the army that can help me, it's here."

Dad took his hand off my shoulder and ran it over my face. He said he would wait for me in the car, and that if he went anywhere he'd call me. He said I had nothing to worry about because he and Mom were behind me, and that whatever happened—and this was something I should know in general for the rest of my life—they would always be with me and would help me in whatever way they could.

II.
***

The guard at the gate asked me what I was there for. I told him I was going to see the MHO, and he asked if I had a referral. I took out the piece of paper folded in four from my pocket, and he smiled and said he was just a soldier and I didn't have to show him the referral because he believed me. I remember his face, his ball-shaped nose, nasal voice, big black eyes, beard.

It was a short walk to the mental health center, and when I got there I found a gray building with a large glass door. Next to the door stood a few soldiers, and when I asked why they were waiting and if we could go in yet, they said soon, and that I should sit down because it would probably take a few minutes.

I sat down on a metal bench near the door. There was quiet music playing in my earphones, and I could hear the other soldiers planning how to get what they wanted out of the MHO. One soldier said he was planning to drool so the MHO would let him go home every afternoon at one. Another waved his hand dismissively and said he'd already tried that and it didn't work.

"No, no, no, bro," the first one said, "I know someone who did it and he got whatever he wanted."

"What do you mean, whatever he wanted?"

"What do I mean whatever he wanted?" the first one

repeated, "I mean the MHO saw him drooling and crying and said: 'Tell me what you want and I'll give it to you.' Just like that, I'm not shitting you. 'Whatever you want!'"

"Bunch of stories," said the skeptical soldier, "everyone's got stories. I know all that. It's all bull, it doesn't work."

"Bro, this is someone reliable," the first one said, but it was clear he was just trying to convince himself at this point.

"Forget it," the skeptic replied with a pitiful look, "forget it."

Then they talked about sports for a while, and about how yesterday one of them was at a party and a girl hit on him but he wasn't interested.

"Why not?" asked the skeptic, and there was something in his tone that sounded as though no woman had ever hit on him, and so he couldn't understand how the other guy could have passed on the opportunity.

"I wasn't into her," the first one explained with self-importance, and judging by his face, which was ugly and dumb, I couldn't believe him. Once I would have scorned him silently, maybe even let out a snort of contempt, but now, on the metal bench, with my stomach contracting and my toes sweating with anxiety and fear, I couldn't be bothered with any of that. I felt no less pathetic than him.

Some of the soldiers were laughing or talking on their phones. Other than me there was only one guy sitting alone quietly. I sank into the bench and looked around at the peeling walls adorned with ridiculous pictures. I felt bad. I felt that I didn't belong to this group of soldiers who had come to get things out of the MHO. I really was miserable in the army, I thought to myself. I really did need the MHO to help me. I really couldn't go back there. Then I thought maybe it would be better to get up and leave, or maybe it would be better to put a bullet through my head and be done with the whole thing, with all this lousy waiting around, and the fear I was doing everything to suppress—the fear that even the MHO wouldn't believe me and I'd have to go back to the base as defeated as I'd arrived. But my body wouldn't move. When Dad called to ask what was happening, I said I didn't know and maybe I should come back to the car. "And what will happen tomorrow?" he asked, with that wonderful ability of his to see the whole picture and disconnect from his personal desires, because I knew that what he really wanted was for me not to go into the MHO and to go back home with him, to go back to the base tomorrow and forget about this whole crappy episode.

"You're right," I said quietly, perhaps defeated, stripped bare of any shred of a possibility of choice. I wanted to cry, but I told myself that there was nothing to cry about now, and that this was the place where they were supposed to help me. I didn't want to get out of the army, and to be honest, as I'd felt all throughout my service, I didn't know what I wanted at all. I didn't have the capacity to know what was good and what wasn't good, or rather, what was bad and what was less bad, where I should go and where I shouldn't. Almost every time someone told me about a particular place that was good, it turned out to be nonsense. And so I sat there on the bench, dazed by all the thoughts ground down into dust, until a female soldier with brown hair and a broken nose came out and said we could start going in.

At the front desk they asked for the referral from my unit physician and the commander's evaluation letter. They gave me a form to fill out. "Sit down, we'll call you," the brown-haired soldier said when I handed her back the form I'd filled in with red pen and asked, "What do I do now?"

I sank back onto one of the metal benches and tapped the floor nervously with my feet.

III.

After a few minutes I heard my name. A tall man in a gray T-shirt and faded jeans smiled at me and motioned for me to follow him. He held a green cardboard file with my name written on it with a red marker. His gait was light and energetic, and when I walked behind him, heavy and tired, I looked at him, trying to extract any crumb of information about this man who was about to condemn my soul—meaning me—to life or death. It was no simple turn of phrase, "life or death," but a cutting fact, dry like dead skin on the soles of your feet.

I looked at his clothes. Young for his age, I thought. An appearance meant to project warmth, maybe to encourage openness or arouse pleasant feelings, unauthoritative, nonmilitary. Then I looked at his haircut, with a part in the middle that seemed to be there to hide his age, which was apparent in the puffiness under his very round eyes.

"Wait outside for just a moment," he said when we got to the office door, and he shut it in my face. I was tense. I thought this was the only place that could restore me to a state of sanity. I don't know if sanity is the right word. Maybe to a state of humanness, of being a normal person, as I was before the horrible enlistment day at the bus station in Haifa, when we stood there with the whole family, and Ayala and Dror and Michal and Michael, and they all hugged me, and

Mom and Michal cried, and Ayala, who was wearing the cut-off shirt she wore on the day we met, hugged me tight, and Dad told me it wasn't easy but I had to get through it and there was no choice.

Then the thought jumped into my head again: What if he didn't believe me? What if he thought I was just another guy who made up stories to get some kind of dispensation? What would happen if even this journey led to nothing, this mental health center, all the hopes I'd pinned on this old, gray clinic? The fear that flooded me made me repress those thoughts immediately and violently. I stood there for a few more minutes, looking at the wooden door with a plain plastic handle, until he suddenly opened it, tall, smiling, even cheerful. I didn't understand what he had to be so cheerful about, and I certainly didn't understand what on earth that celebratory mood was doing in such a place of sorrow and pain.

"Come in," he said, and gestured at a green chair on the near side of the desk. On the other side sat a woman: black hair, red lipstick, red sweater. "I'm David and this is Michal," he chirped, "David and Michal. I keep dancing, and she makes fun of me." He sat down on the chair next to hers and laughed to himself. "Biblical joke," he said, "don't you know that story?" I thought about how I hate those people who, the minute they see a man with a yarmulke, come out with something about the Bible or Judaism, just to show that they know.

"I do," I muttered, impatient with these stupid diversions while my soul was on trial.

"Michal is your mental health officer," he said after a pause. "If you need anything else after today, remember that you go directly to her."

"And you?" I asked.

"Me?" he said, laughing for no reason I could discern, "I'm the clinic director."

Then they talked between themselves for a couple of minutes. It was apparent that she was new, and that he was teaching her the procedures, because he kept showing her what to fill in on the forms and how. The whole time I waited, my legs were shaking and I felt as if there were electrical currents going through my feet.

"So tell us why you're here," said David in a gentle voice, and I don't know if I thought this at the time, but today it's clear that it was just for show. Again I was faced with the problem of how to explain things that can't be put into words. Again I didn't know how to explain the stomachaches every Sunday, the fears, the desire to jump in front of a car or shatter my hand or foot. Again I could not explain the nausea I felt every time I entered the base, the vomiting on Saturday nights and the long hours spent crying in the synagogue.

"I don't know where to start," I said.

"From the beginning," he said, and I thought how trite and pathetic that line was.

"Yes," I said, "from the beginning," wondering what the beginning was. "So the beginning," I said after a moment, "is that I joined a combat unit and did basic training for combat until they discovered I had asthma and transferred me to Intelligence, and that's where everything went wrong, and I don't really know how to explain what went wrong or how, but I just know that I can't tolerate the situation there. My soul can't tolerate it."

"What do you mean, can't tolerate it?" asked David, and I had the feeling he was scolding me for saying something so conclusive.

"Like I said, I'm just overcome with fear and severe pain in my stomach and my heart when I'm there, and I get to states where . . . " Here I fell silent.

"I have to know what your problem is in order to treat it, don't I?" David said after a few seconds. "Come on then, try to define it more specifically."

"I can't tell you a specific problem, I really can't. I just know that that place, that base, those people, the air of that place, all of it . . . that I can't be there. I want to, I mean, I'm asking you to transfer me somewhere else, I'm really asking you." After a pause I added, "I don't know how I can go back there."

I remember now that his face remained indifferent to all my pleas. I remember the part in the middle of his hair, and his big eyes. Nothing moved in them. He repeated the same questions about why I felt the way I did, and asked again that I explain exactly what problems I had "there," meaning on the base. I repeated that I couldn't explain it, and I recounted the long sleepless nights, the pain, the desire to be injured so I could get leave, the frustration of walking around with a trash bag when it was raining and picking up cigarette butts, the feeling of suffocation. "And to tell you the truth," I said, "apart from the actual need to leave that base, there isn't really anything I can put my finger on. There's nothing particular that is the reason for this pain, for this extremely strong need to leave that place."

The conversation in that small room, which was painted white, with all sorts of pictures of Michal with her family, like in any office, is very blurry in my memory. Over and over again I try to replay all the verbiage that was uttered, word for word. Over and over again I try to reconstruct the looks, the tone of voice, but all I can remember is exactly the same questions asked repeatedly, and the cadence that became sterner as the conversation went on. It's an interesting thing the way the soul edits our memory for us, I think to myself—the way it filters out things it finds unnecessary. The way sometimes a person remembers one moment but not the preceding moment or the following one.

IV.

The conclusion of the meeting, which came when David realized I couldn't say anything more than I already had, is something I do remember clearly. After a brief silence, he asked me to wait outside until they called me. I remember his tone: businesslike, unfriendly. Not wisecracking like before, as though he didn't want to create an atmosphere of consolation or hope, like a woman who has made up her mind to leave and doesn't want to give her man the wrong impression.

I also remember Michal's face. It lacked any emotion of its own. Every few moments she looked at David to see what expression was on his face, and then she put the exact same one on hers. Once again, I sat heavily on a metal bench in the hallway. I remember my feet drumming nervously on the floor, I remember an electric shock going through my feet, I remember my heart constricting.

After a few moments they called me back in. The air in the room was still and their faces were impervious. "Look"—I remember David's firm voice—"to be honest, there's not much we can do with you. We've heard what you have to say, but you have to understand that we don't have the authority to transfer a soldier. You see, we're mental health, not the adjutancy, not for your unit and definitely not for the whole army."

I remember my heart sinking—actually crashing into my stomach. I bit my lip as I listened to the words coming out of his big, menacing mouth. I remember the disappointment that flooded me and climbed up my throat. "But can't you write . . ." I tried, but he cut me off like an impatient slaughterer who's already seen hundreds of thousands of chickens pass in front of him with pleading eyes: "No. We can't. We simply have no way of transferring you."

"But I can't go back there," I said.

His face turned severe. "Tell me," he said suddenly, as if he'd just remembered something, "do you even want to do your army service at all?"

"Yes," I replied, "if I didn't want to serve I'd ask to get out, wouldn't I?"

"And do you think you're capable of it, mentally?"

"Yes."

"Then you must know that a soldier doesn't decide where he serves or in what conditions. You do know that, right?" My heart pounded and my tongue froze. "Do you know that?" he asked again. I gave a feeble nod. "If that move you made with your head means yes, and if you want to, and you think you can keep serving in the army, then you have to serve wherever you're posted."

"But there are loads of places in the army," I tried, making an exhausted attempt to fight for logic. "And if I want to serve it doesn't mean it has to be there. I don't understand: If a person wants to serve, like everyone else, why can't he get help with that?"

"Look," he said with an impatience that, in retrospect, I interpret as just another act, like his friendliness at the beginning and his severity in the middle, "I'll say it again: we are not the adjutancy and not human resources. We are mental health. See?" He gestured at the room: "This is the mental health building, and I told you, either you want to get out of the army and you think you're not capable of doing it and that it's damaging you, etc., or you go back to your unit like any other soldier. We are going to write a letter for you now that recommends being as considerate of you as possible. That's the most we can do."

"What do you mean, considerate?" I wanted to cry but I couldn't. "They won't do anything with that. They clearly said they wouldn't transfer me anywhere if there wasn't a strong recommendation from the MHO."

"And I'm telling you again," he said, "this is the most we can do."

Then there was a silence, and he dictated the letter to Michal: "Recommend adjusting mental profile to rank of forty-five. Radicalism in thought, childishness, narcissism. Please allow for the soldier's condition." My legs ached; I had unbearable pressure in my calves. I was weak and my hands were sweating. I thought about an animated film, *Samson the Hero*, which Mom bought me on video when I was a little boy and I watched over and over and over again. I remembered Samson's love for Delilah and all the times she tried to discover the secret to his strength, using all sorts of ruses, and the scene in the film where he killed two hundred and fifty warriors with a donkey's jawbone. Then I remembered the movie's ending, when the Philistines displayed Samson proudly in their palace after they'd captured him: his hair was shaved and he was powerless and defeated. The crowds came to see the lion that had become a lamb, and they made fun of him and poured wine on his face and booed him, and Samson asked God to give him strength one last time. Just one more time, so he could avenge all those who had humiliated him and thereby debased the name of the Lord. Then he spread out his arms and toppled the palace on top of everyone inside it.

I looked at David and Michal again. I silently recited a verse from Psalms, then practically yelled at them: "My blood will be on your hands!" I told David, "My blood will be on your hands," the way I'd said it to Dror on the beach that day when he'd refused to break my hand. "If you force me to go back there even though I'm telling you honestly that I can't go back there, then my blood will be on your hands. I'm telling you—it's on your hands."

I felt my gut turning inside out and I saw his eyes lift up from the paper and he looked at me. There was something frightening in his gaze, as though he could have strangled me.

"What did you say?" he asked with restrained anger.

"I said my blood will be on your hands. I said I can't go back there. I just can't. Why does it have to be so complicated?"

He sat quietly for a few moments and looked down at the desk. Then he looked up and said softly, "If you can't go back there then I'm discharging you from the army."

I remember the blow those words delivered to me, like a powerful punch in the windpipe. I wasn't such an idealist that serving in the army seemed sacred, but still, the possibility of getting out of the army was not something I could consider. Getting out of life, yes. But not out of the army.

"What does it have to do with getting out of the army?" I asked, and I realized my previous statement hadn't toppled any palaces or killed any people.

"If you can't go back there, as you say, then it seems you really can't serve in the army," he declared, and he told Michal to throw away the form and start a new one recommending that I be declared mentally unfit and discharged.

I remember the fear and stress that filled me. I remember seeing Dad's face in my mind's eye as I imagined telling him that I'd been discharged. I remember the sharp pain that cleaved my heart over and over again.

"But I don't want to get out of the army," I said with my last remaining strength. "I really don't."

"In that case," he said, "I will repeat this for the last time: either you go back to your base with the recommendation we're writing and you tolerate it, or we're discharging you."

"I don't want to get out of the army," I repeated. I was defeated, humiliated.

"Then can you go back there?" he asked. "Will you sur-vive there?" As he spoke, I noticed him signaling for Michal to resume with the previous form, the one he'd told her to throw away. He continued to dictate the first recommenda-tion, and when she'd finished he told me to wait for a few more minutes so that Michal could photocopy it and give it to me.

I don't remember Michal's face when she handed me the letter. I was dumbstruck. All I wanted to do was cry. I remember my feet walking toward the exit, striking the old floor tiles heavily. I remember the sight of the other soldiers laughing or staring into space, and all sorts of people in civil-ian clothes walking with cups of coffee or medical files in their hands. Everything was like an old silent movie: sound-less. Very pale colors.

V.

When I was a boy I was often afraid that I had pinworms. I could feel them, or rather I could feel my anus itching and prickling and I thought it was worms, and I was scared they would eat me from the inside. I probably once heard an adult saying that if you eat a lot of chocolate you get worms in your rear end. That's what they used to say in front of us children: rear end. I remember how I'd scratch hard and try to get them out of me, or at least kill them. I remember a bothersome pain that was impossible to ignore, the kind that radiates through the body. Like an earache that hurts your throat too, and your head and sometimes even your neck. I remember having frequent earaches as a child, and every time my ears hurt I would go to Mom and Dad's bed, and I would wake Dad up and tell him I couldn't sleep because of the pain, and he would get up and warm the ear drops and put them in my ears, one in each, and then he would stroke my back until I fell asleep.

That's how I felt then too on my way out of the mental health building, on the big base that was full of trees and buildings and trailers and signs, and the insignia of various units, and soldiers walking like mice inside a huge cage. It was a violent pain, like the worms. But this time it wasn't worms and they weren't in my rear end, but huge lumps of pain inside my stomach, hitting me from inside, exploding all over my body.

I remember how I stood on the square outside the building and the sun hit my face. I felt the need to urinate, and I wanted to eat, and my face was dry and I wanted to put my head under a faucet and wet my hair. At first I thought of going back inside to use the bathroom and wash my face, but when I turned around and saw the glass door and the "Mental Health" sign in big green letters, and next to them the Medical Corps insignia with the snake and sword, I couldn't go in. My feet started pulling me, as if by force, toward the gate I'd entered through that morning, after a sleepless night, hoping that someone here would help me stop being afraid of the army, hoping that here they could give me back my ability to sit in a room and listen to music without my heart sinking every time the army crept into my thoughts. I thought that on the way home I'd ask Dad to stop somewhere, and we could eat and I could use the bathroom and together we'd think about what to do.

"What to do," I think now. As if there were something we hadn't done before I got to the MHO, at the end of my rope, my soul riddled with holes.

.VI.

At the gate, my feet froze. I suddenly realized I couldn't leave in that state, without knowing what was going to happen the next day. Or more accurately, knowing exactly what would happen the next day—that I would have to go back to that cursed base which the law of this country compelled me to be on, and to start the pain and the bad feelings all over again. I stood next to the guard and pictured the bus stop outside the base, and the entry and the mess hall and the barracks and the synagogue and the looks on the faces of the soldiers and the lieutenant colonel and the first lieutenant, Dan. I imagined him asking me—in a teasing voice or a reproachful one—whether the MHO had ended up saying I was fine, which would mean that everything I'd said about how I couldn't do it and I felt horrible was just an act.

Then I remembered that day when I went to the base near Nablus so that Dan could write the evaluation for the MHO, and how everyone who knew me looked at me like I was crazy. The thoughts chased one another at a mad pace. I was already picturing the soldiers sitting on the benches outside the office, laughing at the nutcase whose gun was taken away because he wanted to put a bullet through his head. I could already hear that soldier whom the lieutenant colonel had woken up that night, when I was crumpled next to the green trash can, telling them all how he got woken up and told to take my weapon away, and how he saw me crying. I could already hear him saying that I cried like a cunt, and that right from the start, back when he pranked me and sent me out at midnight to sign off on some equipment at the quartermaster's and I believed him, he knew I was screwed up. Then I could hear how everyone laughed and he repeated: "Like a cunt, I'm telling you, like a total cunt."

I pictured the paths on the base, which get muddy in winter, and I pictured the minutes before morning roll call. I saw myself jumping off the top bunk and quickly getting dressed and shoving my feet into my boots. I remembered the verse from Psalms that I would whisper as the drill sergeant passed among the soldiers to see if anyone's boots were slightly dirty, and the inconceivable fear that he would call on me and send me to polish my boots and then report to his office, and that he'd judge me and maybe make me stay on the base for Shabbat.

I raised my head and looked at the guard again. It wasn't the same soldier from the morning; instead there was a blond female soldier smoking a cigarette. I looked at the cars parked outside and thought how lucky it was that Dad hadn't found a parking spot near the gate, because I didn't want to leave yet and abandon my fate to hell, and if he'd parked closer then he'd have already seen me standing there and he'd probably get out of the car and ask what had happened, and he'd put his hand on my shoulder or stroke my cheek and say there was nothing left to do, there was no point hanging around here, we should go home, there was no choice, I'd have to try again and see how I handled it.

VII.

I turned around and went back. My bladder was pressing and I went to look for a toilet. After I peed, I sat down on a bench and stared into space. I can't go home like this, I thought to myself. I looked at two female soldiers walking arm in arm. I wanted to call Ayala. I suddenly missed her high-pitched voice. I wanted to hear her say that she'd always be there for me, no matter what happened. I wanted to tell her about everything that happened with the MHO, and about how even he didn't help me, and that I didn't know what to do and my stomach ached with despair.

I suddenly felt a strong need to tell her I loved her, to just get those words out to someone, to her. To tell her that I wanted to marry her. Here, now, without any romance or drama. To just be with her throughout this life.

I knew she'd probably say, again, that I had to get out of this stinking army and start my life, and that I shouldn't let this country destroy me, and that it didn't make sense that a country that was supposed to protect me should destroy me like this. She'd say that if the MHO had offered me a discharge, I should go back in and tell him that's what I wanted. Then she'd probably say that, as for getting married, we'd do it "when the time comes." *When the time comes.* She always liked those poetic phrases.

"Some people die in battle and some people die on a bench

outside the MHO." That's the sentence that came to mind when I thought about what I would tell her, and I imagined her laughing. I enjoyed imagining her laughing. I remembered how on my eighteenth birthday we were on the beach, and she hugged me from behind and said that from now on I could do whatever I wanted. She asked if "when the time comes" I would take her as my wife. I remembered the innocence I felt in my gut when I heard those words. Now I think how hollow they were and how much dishonesty they contained.

I didn't call her, because when I took my phone out of my pocket and looked at it, I no longer wanted to call. I even felt a slight disgust, the way I felt once when I sat in a cafe next to Ayala and her profile suddenly looked ugly. I put the phone back in my pocket. Dad phoned a minute later and I told him I was still waiting and it would take a while longer. He said he was outside. I stared into space and for a long moment I didn't think about anything, and every time I let a thought steal into my head, I was immediately overcome with fear and a strong desire to die. A group of noisy soldiers walking by reminded me again of that horrible base and everything that was bad about it, as if I hadn't been thinking of it the whole time.

Those moments outside the mental health building passed inexorably, and I knew I had to decide. I felt as if my choice was between death and . . . I didn't honestly know what the other option was. I couldn't go back to that base, and I couldn't, in my mind, go AWOL or defect, because I knew that then I would live in constant fear that they'd come and find me and put me in prison, and the thing I wanted least of all was to keep running away. I wanted a clear decision: life or death. I wanted them to tell me if they were sending me to die or not. Then I realized that in fact they had told me; they'd already abandoned me.

I kept mulling over these ideas, and I even thought about convenient ways of dying, like taking pills or jumping off a tower, options that didn't involve too much pain, until suddenly, and I write "suddenly" because no matter how much I try to reconstruct the moment and understand how it happened, I cannot, it was as though the lust to live—such a big phrase for such a miserable, banal thing—took over, and I stood up and walked into the building. There was nothing heroic or brave about that walk. It was heavy, and my eyes— or so I felt—were half-shut.

VIII.

I remember walking up the stairs. I remember the floor tiles I stepped on one after the other on the way to the office. I was empty. I knew this was my last chance. I thought about Samson again, and his face in the cartoon when he asks God to give him strength just one last time. I saw how he stretched his arms out to the sides and strained his face and brought the palace columns down on himself and everyone around him.

When I finished recalling the movie scene, at the moment the palace columns shattered, I found myself standing outside the plain wooden door with Michal the MHO's name on it. I knocked twice, softly, and I remember her voice responding with a tired "Yes." I opened the door and went in. I stood facing her. "Yes?" she repeated, looking up from a paper.

I told her I'd been there a little over an hour ago, maybe an hour and a half, with David.

"Yes, yes, I remember," she said quickly before I could finish. "What's wrong?"

"Can I sit down?" I asked. I could feel my legs about to buckle.

"Actually," she said, "I have a meeting in fifteen minutes, so just for a few moments, okay?"

I nodded. I explained that I'd come back because I just couldn't leave knowing that I had to go back to that base tomorrow. I told her again about the feelings I had and about how I wanted to serve in the army and I wasn't trying to get out of it or make my life easy, and that I'd really tried to get along on that base, "God, how I tried," but I felt that I could not go back there. It was as simple as that: I could not go back.

"David already told you that we have no way to help you with that," she said, repeating the same empty words about how they weren't the adjutancy, and they couldn't force my unit to transfer me, and they could only make a recommendation.

"But I can't go back there," I suddenly shouted, to make her stop talking. "I really can't go back there. I'm not lying. I'm really not lying." I put my head down on the desk. "I can't go back there," I kept saying through my tears, "I can't."

"Maybe you can't serve in the army," she said, trying that trick again, talking quietly, almost maternally.

I felt I no longer had anything to lose, so I answered softly, "I can serve in the army. I just can't serve there. What's so hard to get about that? What's so complicated? Why make things complicated all the time? I just can't go back there. I just can't."

And like that, with my head on the desk, sobbing, I sat there and murmured to myself over and over again that I couldn't go back to the base. Michal said nothing and I felt her looking at me and evaluating how genuine my behavior was. I silently recited the Psalms verses I'd learned by heart and felt that I might vomit on the floor at any minute. "A song of ascents," I mouthed, "I will lift up mine eyes unto the mountains: From whence shall my help come? My help cometh from the Lord, who made heaven and earth. He will not suffer thy foot to be moved. He that keepeth thee will not slumber. Behold, he that keepeth Israel doth neither slumber nor sleep. The Lord is thy keeper; the Lord is thy shade upon thy right hand. The sun shall not smite thee by day, nor the moon by night. The Lord shall keep thee from all evil; He shall keep thy soul. The Lord shall guard thy going out and thy coming in, from this time forth and forever." Then I recited more verses: "Lord, who shall sojourn in Thy tabernacle?" and "Keep me, O God; for I have taken refuge in Thee," and I rolled the words around in my mind and maybe on my lips, over and over again, until suddenly Michal sighed. There was something sad about her sigh, about the way she let the air out of her mouth and the sound she made. I felt her gazing at me more tenderly than she had before, and I looked up at her face.

"You won't have to go back there," she said suddenly. I don't remember exactly how it happened, and I can't put my finger on looks or tones of voice or expressions, but looking back, it seems to me as though a holy spirit entered the room and enveloped me and Michal and the whole moment. She said she would talk to my base and inform them that I wasn't going back, and that meanwhile I'd be at home and she'd give me as much sick leave as it took until they realized I couldn't be there and transferred me back to the induction center, where they'd post me somewhere new, close to home, and she hoped it would be a place where I could serve without having all these bad feelings. Then she said that as long as she was giving me sick leave, I had to come see her once a week, and that each time I came she would give me a form with sick leave for the following week, because she couldn't give me more than a week's worth at once. Then she asked if I had the phone number of the adjutancy on my base so that she could talk to whoever was in charge there, and I gave her the biggest grin I was capable of, which was a pretty pathetic one, and said I had the number because we'd used it a lot recently—me and Dad and of course Mom, who'd called more than anyone involved in this story. I read her the number from my phone and she said I should go wash my face, and meanwhile she'd talk to them, and that while she did that she would print out my sick leave for the coming week.

IX.

I remember standing in the little bathroom of the mental health clinic, splashing my face with more and more water. I remember looking into my eyes, which were red from lack of sleep and from all the pain I had endured. I hadn't looked at my eyes for a long time, I realized, and I remembered that once I used to look at my eyes a lot to see if they really had any green inside the brown, as girls had told me. For the first time in ages, I dared to look for that green again.

I did everything like a machine. With ridiculous caution, as if I was afraid to do something reckless that would change the reality that had suddenly been created after I'd all but given up. As if I were afraid that I'd fallen asleep on the desk while I was crying and at any moment I'd wake up and realize that everything that was said in that room was a lie, a fantasy. I'd had similar fantasies before, dreams in which everything somehow got resolved, in which I no longer felt the terrible pain that was eating away at my stomach and giving me no peace. Now someone had finally understood that I was really in a bad state and that I wasn't lying. I remembered a day-dream I'd had while I was waiting on the bench outside the camp commander's office. I remembered the sharp pain that pierced my stomach when I roused and saw his office and saw myself in my dirty uniform, waiting for him.

X.

_____

When I went back to Michal's office, she was waiting for me with a cup of coffee. The sick leave form was in the printer tray. "I talked to them," she said, in a tone that was part reassuring, part proud. "I told them that as long as they don't get you out of there to the Chief Adjutancy, you won't be going back to the base, and that I'm responsible for it." She reached out to the printer and gave me the form, and reminded me that I had to come see her once a week, "So we can talk and so I can give you sick leave for the next week."

"I remember," I said. Then I said, "Thank you very much," and I left the room and the building. Outside, the same sun was still hanging, perhaps even stronger. I stood looking at that base, at the bench I'd sat on half an hour earlier thinking about the best way to commit suicide, at the white buildings, at the black asphalt paths. I didn't have any feelings of happiness or victory or revenge. Whom could I feel victorious over? All I felt, for the first time in a long time, was tranquility. Calmness. Calmness from the simple knowledge that I would not have to go back to the base, and from the even simpler fact that for the coming week I would be at home. I could visit Ayala, and I would finally be able to sit and read a book without struggling to suppress thoughts about the army while I read. I felt that after a long time I could breathe like a human being—just breathe. Then I thought about Dror and I called to tell him that I'd be on leave all week, and I asked if he wanted to take a trip. "Maybe to the Kinneret," I said, "like we did the week before I enlisted." He asked why I was on leave, and I said they'd found some breathing difficulties related to the asthma, and that there was a good chance I'd be at home a lot in the near future.

Then I called Ayala. I told her about the leave and the asthma, and I asked if she wanted to meet me during the week. I didn't want to tell her about the MHO. I was no longer sure we were going to be together forever, and I was afraid that if we broke up she would tell other people about it. I suppose our relationship was already dead, and the final separation, which came a few months later, was only a memorial service for the corpse we were already carrying around.

Then I walked out and got into Dad's car. On the way out, I glanced at a group of soldiers standing by the snack bar licking ice cream. "How was it?" Dad asked, turning to look at me. I told him everything that had happened, and how in the end, thank God, it had all worked out, and that Michal had promised me I wouldn't go back to that base anymore. "What do you mean, you won't go back there anymore?" he asked, and I told him about the whole thing with the sick leave until they transferred me to the Chief Adjutancy. Then he asked what they'd written on the evaluation and I handed him the form. He read it closely, then looked at me. "You really are a bit of a narcissist," he said. He laughed, and I realized I hadn't seen him laugh for a long time.

"Do you think it's problematic, the mental health ranking?" I asked him.

"I don't know. It could be . . . " He paused for a moment. "Either way, you can be sure that if any problems come up, we'll be with you, and we'll try to help you as much as we can."

He started the car and turned his head back to reverse out of the parking spot. The Leonard Cohen CD started playing from the beginning, and the cup of coffee Dad had drunk on the way sat empty in the cup holder. The sun shone powerfully and lit up the street. The silent houses were the same ones that had stood there when we'd arrived that morning, and when I'd lingered by the gate before deciding to go back in.

YAIR ASSULIN, born in 1986, studied philosophy and history at the Hebrew University in Jerusalem. *The Drive* is the first of two novels he has written and for which he won Israel's Ministry of Culture Prize and the Sapir Prize for debut fiction. He has been awarded the Prime Minister's Prize for authors, writes a weekly column in the newspaper *Haaretz* and has been a visiting lecturer in Jewish studies at Yale.

JESSICA COHEN shared the 2017 Man Booker International Prize with author David Grossman for her translation of *A Horse Walks into a Bar*. She has translated works by Amos Oz, Etgar Keret, Dorit Rabinyan, Ronit Matalon and Nir Baram.

AND THE BRIDE CLOSED THE DOOR
BY RONIT MATALON

A young bride shuts herself up in a bedroom on her wedding day, refusing to get married. In this moving and humorous look at contemporary Israel and the chaotic ups and downs of love everywhere, her family gathers outside the locked door, not knowing what to do. The only communication they receive from behind the door are scribbled notes, one of them a cryptic poem about a prodigal daughter returning home. The harder they try to reach the defiant woman, the more the despairing groom is convinced that her refusal should be respected. But what, exactly, ought to be respected? Is this merely a case of cold feet?

SOME DAY
BY SHEMI ZARHIN

On the shores of Israel's Sea of Galilee lies the city of Tiberias, a place bursting with sexuality and longing for love. The air is saturated with smells of cooking and passion. *Some Day* is a gripping family saga, a sensual and emotional feast that plays out over decades. This is an enchanting tale about tragic fates that disrupt families and break our hearts. Zarhin's hypnotic writing renders a painfully delicious vision of individual lives behind Israel's larger national story.

ALEXANDRIAN SUMMER
BY YITZHAK GORMEZANO GOREN

This is the story of two Jewish families living their frenzied last days in the doomed cosmopolitan social whirl of Alexandria just before fleeing Egypt for Israel in 1951. The conventions of the Egyptian upper-middle class are laid bare in this dazzling novel, which exposes sexual hypocrisies and portrays a vanished polyglot world of horse racing, seaside promenades and nightclubs.

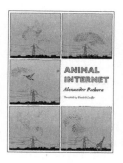

ANIMAL INTERNET
BY ALEXANDER PSCHERA

Some 50,000 creatures around the globe—including whales, leopards, flamingoes, bats and snails—are being equipped with digital tracking devices. The data gathered and studied by major scientific institutes about their behavior will warn us about tsunamis, earthquakes and volcanic eruptions, but also radically transform our relationship to the natural world. Contrary to pessimistic fears, author Alexander Pschera sees the Internet as creating a historic opportunity for a new dialogue between man and nature.

EXPOSED
BY JEAN-PHILIPPE BLONDEL

A dangerous intimacy emerges between a French teacher and a former student who has achieved art world celebrity. The painting of a portrait upturns both their lives. Jean-Philippe Blondel, author of the bestselling novel *The 6:41 to Paris,* evokes an intimacy of dangerous intensity in a stunning tale about aging, regret and moving ahead into the future.

THE 6:41 TO PARIS
BY JEAN-PHILIPPE BLONDEL

Cécile, a stylish 47-year-old, has spent the weekend visiting her parents outside Paris. By Monday morning, she's exhausted. These trips back home are stressful and she settles into a train compartment with an empty seat beside her. But it's soon occupied by a man she recognizes as Philippe Leduc, with whom she had a passionate affair that ended in her brutal humiliation 30 years ago. In the fraught hour and a half that ensues, Cécile and Philippe hurtle towards the French capital in a psychological thriller about the pain and promise of past romance.

OBLIVION
BY SERGEI LEBEDEV

In one of the first 21st century Russian novels to probe the legacy of the Soviet prison camp system, a young man travels to the vast wastelands of the Far North to uncover the truth about a shadowy neighbor who saved his life, and whom he knows only as Grandfather II. Emerging from today's Russia, where the ills of the past are being forcefully erased from public memory, this masterful novel represents an epic literary attempt to rescue history from the brink of oblivion.

THE YEAR OF THE COMET
BY SERGEI LEBEDEV

A story of a Russian boyhood and coming of age as the Soviet Union is on the brink of collapse. Lebedev depicts a vast empire coming apart at the seams, transforming a very public moment into something tender and personal, and writes with stunning beauty and shattering insight about childhood and the growing consciousness of a boy in the world.

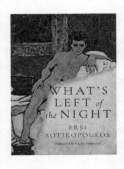

WHAT'S LEFT OF THE NIGHT
BY ERSI SOTIROPOULOS

Constantine Cavafy arrives in Paris in 1897 on a trip that will deeply shape his future and push him toward his poetic inclination. With this lyrical novel, tinged with an hallucinatory eroticism that unfolds over three unforgettable days, celebrated Greek author Ersi Sotiropoulos depicts Cavafy in the midst of a journey of self-discovery across a continent on the brink of massive change. A stunning portrait of a budding author—before he became C.P. Cavafy, one of the 20th century's greatest poets—that illuminates the complex relationship of art, life, and the erotic desires that trigger creativity.

THE EYE
BY PHILIPPE COSTAMAGNA

It's a rare and secret profession, comprising a few dozen people around the world equipped with a mysterious mixture of knowledge and innate sensibility. Summoned to Swiss bank vaults, Fifth Avenue apartments, and Tokyo storerooms, they are entrusted by collectors, dealers, and museums to decide if a coveted picture is real or fake and to determine if it was painted by Leonardo da Vinci or Raphael. *The Eye* lifts the veil on the rarified world of connoisseurs devoted to the authentication and discovery of Old Master artworks.

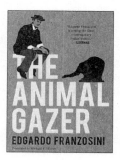

THE ANIMAL GAZER
BY EDGARDO FRANZOSINI

A hypnotic novel inspired by the strange and fascinating life of sculptor Rembrandt Bugatti, brother of the fabled automaker. Bugatti obsessively observes and sculpts the baboons, giraffes, and panthers in European zoos, finding empathy with their plight and identifying with their life in captivity. Rembrandt Bugatti's work, now being rediscovered, is displayed in major art museums around the world and routinely fetches large sums at auction. Edgardo Franzosini recreates the young artist's life with intense lyricism, passion, and sensitivity.

ALLMEN AND THE DRAGONFLIES
BY MARTIN SUTER

Johann Friedrich von Allmen has exhausted his family fortune by living in Old World grandeur despite present-day financial constraints. Forced to downscale, Allmen inhabits the garden house of his former Zurich estate, attended by his Guatemalan butler, Carlos. This is the first of a series of humorous, fast-paced detective novels devoted to a memorable gentleman thief. A thrilling art heist escapade infused with European high culture and luxury that doesn't shy away from the darker side of human nature.

THE MADELEINE PROJECT
BY CLARA BEAUDOUX

A young woman moves into a Paris apartment and discovers a storage room filled with the belongings of the previous owner, a certain Madeleine who died in her late nineties, and whose treasured possessions nobody seems to want. In an audacious act of journalism driven by personal curiosity and humane tenderness, Clara Beaudoux embarks on *The Madeleine Project*, documenting what she finds on Twitter with text and photographs, introducing the world to an unsung 20th century figure.

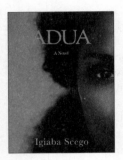

ADUA
BY IGIABA SCEGO

Adua, an immigrant from Somalia to Italy, has lived in Rome for nearly forty years. She came seeking freedom from a strict father and an oppressive regime, but her dreams of film stardom ended in shame. Now that the civil war in Somalia is over, her homeland calls her. She must decide whether to return and reclaim her inheritance, but also how to take charge of her own story and build a future.

IF VENICE DIES
BY SALVATORE SETTIS

Internationally renowned art historian Salvatore Settis ignites a new debate about the Pearl of the Adriatic and cultural patrimony at large. In this fiery blend of history and cultural analysis, Settis argues that "hit-and-run" visitors are turning Venice and other landmark urban settings into shopping malls and theme parks. This is a passionate plea to secure the soul of Venice, written with consummate authority, wide-ranging erudition and élan.